"Are you looking for a soul mate?" Marly's brows rose.

"Oh, hell no," he answered. "What would I do with a soul mate when I'm never in one place long enough to grow roots?"

She nodded. "Exactly." Marly tipped her head toward the plane. "Besides, I have my soul mate." She patted her hand against the plane's fuselage. "He doesn't argue with me much, he sweeps me off my feet and he carries me anywhere I want to go."

Pitbull frowned. "Your plane?"

Marly shrugged. "I don't have to worry about him cheating on me."

"Until another pilot comes along," Pitbull pointed out.

"I don't have to cook for him," Marly continued.

"You have to feed it aviation fuel, which can't be cheap," Pitbull countered.

"He doesn't care what I wear or whether I put on makeup."

"You got me there." Pitbull's lips twitched for a second. He stared at Marly's fresh, clean face and sparkling blue-gray eyes. "But seriously, you don't need makeup."

Marly's cheeks filled with a soft pink color, giving her a more feminine look. "Thanks. And for that, you win the prize."

Pitbull's lips curled into a wry grin. "What prize?"

Marly smiled. "Copilot's seat."

"Are you looking for a tour guide?" Mary's brows rose.

"Oh ball..." he says... "...you would do with a sub..." ...

"...her..."

...

TWO DAUNTLESS HEARTS

―

New York Times Bestselling Author

ELLE JAMES

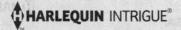

HARLEQUIN INTRIGUE®

This book is dedicated to all the wild animals in Africa that make it such an interesting and beautiful place to visit. Also, to the people who strive to keep those animals safe from poachers. They deserve a chance to live and roam free of harm.

ISBN-13: 978-1-335-63919-6

Two Dauntless Hearts

Copyright © 2018 by Mary Jernigan

PLEASE RECYCLE · THIS PRODUCT IS RECYCLABLE

Recycling programs for this product may not exist in your area.

Printed in U.S.A.

www.Harlequin.com

Elle James, a *New York Times* bestselling author, started writing when her sister challenged her to write a romance novel. She has managed a full-time job and raised three wonderful children, and she and her husband even tried ranching exotic birds (ostriches, emus and rheas). Ask her, and she'll tell you what it's like to go toe-to-toe with an angry 350-pound bird! Elle loves to hear from fans at ellejames@earthlink.net or ellejames.com.

Books by Elle James

Harlequin Intrigue

Mission: Six

One Intrepid SEAL
Two Dauntless Hearts

Ballistic Cowboys

Hot Combat
Hot Target
Hot Zone
Hot Velocity

SEAL of My Own

Navy SEAL Survival
Navy SEAL Captive
Navy SEAL to Die For
Navy SEAL Six Pack

Visit the Author Profile page at Harlequin.com.

CAST OF CHARACTERS

"Pitbull" Percy Taylor—US Navy SEAL, a tough guy who doesn't date much. Raised by a taciturn marine father. Lives by the rules and structure. SOC-R boat captain.

Marly Simpson—Bush pilot in Africa. Her father was a bush pilot and taught her to fly. Her mother teaches children in the poor villages of Africa.

Talia Montclair—Owner/operator of the All Things Wild Safari & Resort in Kenya.

"Diesel" Dalton Samuel Landon—US Navy SEAL. Gunner and team lead.

"Buck" Graham Bucker—US Navy SEAL, team medic. Went to medical school but didn't finish, then joined the navy and became a SEAL.

"Harm" Harmon Payne—US Navy SEAL, light on his feet and fast. Good at silent entry into buildings.

"Big Jake" Jake Schuler—US Navy SEAL, demolitions expert. For a big guy, he's excellent at fine fingerwork.

"T-Mac" Trace McGuire—US Navy SEAL, communications man, equipment expert.

The Boss—Mysterious man with an American accent.

Reverend Eugene Thomas—Missionary working in a small village.

Chapter One

"Nope. I'm not going." One look at the plane
they'd already flown in twice and he was out.
Done. Finished. He put himself in harm's way
too often to risk it on vacation.

Percy "Pitbull" Taylor spun on his heels.
He started back toward the van and the driver
who'd brought six members of his SEAL team
to the small landing strip outside of Camp
Lemonnier on the Horn of Africa. "Twice was
enough. I thought you'd snared a ride with the
160th Night Stalkers. I prefer helicopters. You
know how I feel about crop dusters."

Buck clapped a hand to his shoulder and
turned him back around. "Now, don't go getting your boxers in a twist."

"I don't wear boxers," Pitbull grumbled.

"You've flown with Marly twice. She's
a good pilot and she knows her plane. And

it's not a crop duster. Besides, nothing bad happened on the previous two flights. What makes you think anything will happen this time?"

Pitbull frowned as he let Buck guide him toward the small bush plane they'd used in their last operation to rescue the US Secretary of Defense's son and his hot, tough-as-nails assistant. "Yeah, but three's a charm." He tipped his head toward the offending aircraft. "Look at it. I swear it's only held together by spit and duct tape."

With a low chuckle, Buck leaned closer. "Don't let Marly hear you badmouth her bird. She might decide to leave us behind."

"That would be just fine with me." Pitbull sighed. "I can't believe you talked me into doing this." He shook his head. "I'd have been perfectly happy waiting for our next assignment back at camp."

"Seriously?" Diesel shot a glance over his shoulder as he walked ahead. "You have the chance of a lifetime to go on a safari in Africa, and you'd rather stay at Camp-Hot-As-Hell-in-the-Friggin'-Desert eating MREs?"

"I can't believe the CO granted us leave here in Africa." Harm came up from behind

Pitbull, sliding his backpack over his left shoulder. "Somebody slip something into his drink last night?"

"I think he got a little pressure from the Sec Def," Big Jake said.

"One week." T-Mac grinned back at Pitbull and Harm from where he walked next to Diesel. "One whole week to get a real feel for the majesty of the savanna and experience all the animals we only see in zoos." The man practically skipped toward the plane, his step quickening as if he feared the CO would show up and pull their leave request. T-Mac had a knack with animals. He planned to own a ranch when his gig with the navy was up. He talked nonstop about the horses, cattle, llamas and other exotics he planned to populate the ranch with when he got out.

That was T-Mac.

Pitbull couldn't think past the plane standing in front of him. He much preferred helicopters. Oh, he knew they were more dangerous than planes, but he'd grown accustomed to them. The whopping sound of rotors soothed his anxieties about heights and leaving the ground. The single-engine prop job of an airplane didn't give him the warm fuzzies. Far from it.

As they neared the plane, Pitbull's nerves stretched. He focused on the pilot walking around the exterior, performing preflight checks.

They'd met Marly Simpson a couple weeks ago, when she'd helped them on a mission. They'd needed air transport in a hurry and had been forced to skip the call to their usual helicopter support team. She'd come through in the pinch.

But hell, they weren't in a pinch now. Why the hell did they have to fly in that tin can?

Marly wore a khaki-colored flight suit, the outfit hugging her slender body like a glove, accentuating every curve. The woman was a no-holds-barred, tough gal who could hold her own in any conversation or situation. She flew all over the African continent in that rust bucket, transporting people and cargo to the most inaccessible, dangerous and god-awful places without batting a single pretty eyelash.

Yeah, Pitbull had noticed Marly and the fact she had a sexy, slender neck, ripe for kissing. Her long sandy-blond hair hung down to her waist when she pulled it out of the perpetual ponytail she wore, but that didn't make the fact they were flying in a single-engine prop job to their vacation destination any more appealing to Pitbull. It helped, but not enough.

Marly completed her inspection before they reached her and turned in their direction. "Hi," she said in her unassuming, warm voice, a smile spreading across her face. "Great to see you guys."

Harm reached her first.

Marly held out her hand. "Harm, you're looking well."

"You, too." Harm shook her hand and stood back as she greeted the rest of the team.

Diesel took her outstretched hand and pulled her into a bear hug. "Can't tell you how glad we were when you said you could take us to Kenya."

"My pleasure." She smiled up at Diesel. "How's Reese?"

He gave half a smile. "She's in the States. She promised me a date when I got back."

Marly's lips pressed together. "Long-distance relationships. They can suck."

"Yeah." Diesel shrugged. "But what can you do? If you love someone enough, you can work it out. And I'm not ashamed to admit I'm completely smitten with Reese."

"Never thought I'd hear those words coming out of your mouth." Buck bumped Diesel's shoulder with one of his own. "What changed your mind?"

Diesel laughed. "You have to ask?"

"Reese." Big Jake pushed his way through the rest of the team and hugged Marly. "Guess Diesel found his soul mate, or some other drivel."

Diesel balled his hands into a fist, a fierce frown pulling his brows low. "I take offense to your calling Reese drivel. And since when do you use words like *drivel*?"

"You know I don't mean anything by it," Big Jake said. "I'm just jealous." He hooked his arm over Marly's shoulder. "Will you be my soul mate, Marly? I like an independent badass of a woman."

Pitbull's fists clenched at Big Jake's casual claim on the pretty pilot. Why he should tense when another man made a move on Marly was beyond him. It wasn't as if he had a stake in the game or wanted her for himself. A navy SEAL's life was no place for relationships. Besides, Marly lived and worked in Africa.

Other than the occasional mission, they never saw each other. Again...not that he was interested in seeing Marly.

Although he had to admit, she wasn't bad looking. Maybe a little less womanly than Pitbull's usual feminine fare.

She chortled and threw a light punch into Big Jake's belly. "Is that how you see me? As a badass?"

"Damn right," he replied, rubbing his gut. "Any woman who'd risk flying in and out of some of the most hostile territories in Africa—that alone is downright kickass in my books. And you have a helluva right hook."

She nodded. "I'll take that as a compliment." Tipping her head to the side, she stared up at his six-foot-four-inch frame and narrowed her eyes. "As for being your soul mate, I'll have to think about it." She unhooked Big Jake's arm from around her shoulders and turned to the others. "You can stow your bags in the luggage compartment or behind the back seat inside the plane."

While Diesel, Big Jake, Harm, Buck and T-Mac stowed their gear, Marly turned to Pitbull. "What about you?"

Pitbull's pulse quickened and his brain

scrambled at her direct stare. *Shit.* What was it about this woman that tied him in knots? He squared his shoulders and lifted his chin. "What *about* me?"

"Are you looking for a soul mate?" Marly's brows rose.

"Oh, hell no," he answered. "What would I do with a soul mate when I'm never in one place long enough to grow roots?"

"Exactly." Marly nodded toward the plane. "Besides, I have my soul mate." She patted the plane's fuselage. "He doesn't argue with me much, sweeps me off my feet and carries me anywhere I want to go."

Pitbull frowned. "Your plane?"

Marly shrugged. "I don't have to worry about him cheating on me."

"Until another pilot comes along," Pitbull pointed out.

"I don't have to cook for him," Marly continued.

"You have to feed it aviation fuel, which can't be cheap," Pitbull countered.

"He doesn't care what I wear or whether I put on makeup."

"You got me there." Pitbull's lips twitched for a second. He stared at Marly's fresh, clean face and sparkling blue-gray eyes. "But seriously, you don't need makeup."

Marly's cheeks filled with a soft pink color, giving her a more feminine look. "Thanks. And for that, you win the prize."

Pitbull's lips curled into a wry grin. "What prize?"

Marly smiled. "Copilot's seat." Before Pitbull could protest, she clapped her hands sharply and faced the men standing around the plane. "If you're ready, we can get this show on the road."

"But—" Pitbull started.

Buck pounded Pitbull's back. "Congratulations, you lucky dog. You'll have the best seat on the bus."

"If you like it so much, *you* take it." Pitbull waved a hand toward the plane.

"I wouldn't dream of depriving you of such a prime location." Buck winked at Marly. "I'm sure the pilot will take very good care of you."

"You know damn good and well how I feel about this plane," Pitbull grumbled low enough for Buck to hear without clueing Marly in on their earlier discussion.

Buck cupped the back of his ear. "What's that you say?" His brows rose high, his lips curling into a devilish grin. "You were going to tell Marly how you felt about her pride and joy?" He whacked Pitbull in the back hard enough to send him staggering forward. "Go ahead. Tell her how much you love flying in fixed-wing aircraft." The bastard crossed his arms over his chest and waited.

Marly stared at Pitbull, another smile tugging at her lips.

Caught between Buck's taunts and Marly's expectant stare, he did the only thing he could. He lied. "I can't wait to ride shotgun."

Marly's eyes narrowed briefly. If he hadn't been watching so closely, he would have missed it. But then her face cleared and she grinned. "Great. I'll brief you on how to land this baby in case something happens to me."

Pitbull shot a horrified glance her direction. He ran his gaze from the tip of her toes to the top of her head. "Holy shit, Marly. You aren't expecting to croak while flying, are you?"

She laughed, a throaty, surprisingly sexy sound that caught and held Pitbull's attention, despite her random threat of dying while in flight. His heartbeat ratcheted up and his groin tightened. What the hell? Marly wasn't the kind of woman he usually found attractive.

He went for dark-haired, curvy women who knew how to flirt and didn't expect anything past a one-night stand.

Marly's face lit and her eyes shone. "Don't worry," she said. "I'm as healthy as a horse."

His heart hammering against his ribs, Pitbull forgot to be angry or disconcerted about having to ride in the cockpit of the aircraft. For that moment, he was lost in Marly's laughter and smile.

Damn. This couldn't be good.

He tore his gaze from her fresh face and happy smile to watch, without really "seeing," as his teammates climbed aboard the aircraft and settled into their seats.

"If you're ready," Marly said beside him and touched his arm. "I'll close the door behind us. Really, I'm fine. I won't pass out and die during our flight." She held up her hand. "Scout's honor."

He frowned. "I'm holding you to that promise. And I doubt seriously you were ever a Scout." Then he ascended the steps into the tiny plane. Hunkering low to keep from bumping his head, he passed down the aisle and settled into the copilot's place on the right.

Taking full responsibility for the aircraft,

Marly secured the door behind her and joined him, resting a hand on his shoulder as she lowered herself into her seat.

Where her hand had been remained warm long after she removed it. If he were honest with himself, he'd own up to the tingling sensation sizzling through his body at her touch. Obviously he'd been too long without a woman in his bed. But now was not the time to be thinking of such a thing.

Marly was the pilot, nothing more.

"Buckle up, buttercup," Marly said, fastening her safety straps. Over her shoulder, she told the others, "As you all well know, this isn't your usual jetliner flight. I'll be your pilot, or rather, copilot—with Pitbull's assistance—and flight attendant. Please fasten your seat belts and keep them fastened until we land. There will be no beverages served on this flight, and there is no lavatory." She gave the guys in the back a wicked grin. "If you should need to relieve yourself…hold it until we make our refueling stop halfway there."

"Well, damn," Buck complained. "I wanted a beer."

T-Mac followed with, "And I was really looking forward to the peanuts."

Big Jake waved a dismissive hand. "Ignore the whiners. We're all set. Let 'er rip."

"And by 'let 'er rip,' he means make a smooth takeoff and an even smoother landing," Pitbull mumbled.

"I heard that." Marly's pretty pink lips twisted. She slapped a headset against his chest. "Wear these so you know what's going on."

He slipped the headset over his ears and plugged the wires into the communications ports. "Do I want to know what's going on?"

She leaned back and gave him an assessing stare. "Pitbull, are you telling me you're afraid of a little ol' plane ride?" Her brows rose into the hair swooping down over her brow.

Buck leaned forward. "Bingo! Give the lady a prize."

Marly shook her head. "You have nothing to worry about. I have over three thousand hours flying this plane alone, and more in other types of aircraft. I started flying at thirteen, over fifteen years ago. I think I can handle it." She checked the instrument panel, flicked several switches and started the engine.

As the propeller spun into action, Pitbull's gut clenched.

"Relax. We'll be there before you know it," Marly said into the mic.

Her voice filled the earphones of his headset, reassuring Pitbull when he needed it most.

Marly spoke to the nearby air traffic controller, got her instructions and started the plane taxiing toward the runway. "With all you go through as a navy SEAL, I can't believe you're afraid of flying."

"I'm not afraid of flying," Pitbull said through clenched teeth, his fingers digging into the armrest at his side. "I'm afraid of crashing."

"But you fly in helicopters all the time," Marly reasoned, pushing the throttle forward. The aircraft gained speed as it barreled down the runway.

"I do it as part of the job." Pitbull tensed, praying the runway was long enough. "And helicopters don't eat up thousands of feet of runway to take off."

Still grinning, Marly kept her gaze on the runway ahead. "Yeah, but when the propeller stops, helicopters drop like a rock to the earth. Airplanes, on the other hand, can glide for miles." Just as they neared the end of the runway, the plane left the ground, the wings seesawing slightly as they lifted the craft into the air.

Pitbull leaned back, willing the plane to continue its climb. "Planes can glide for miles, but they still need thousands of feet of runway to land. Helicopters don't. Besides, I'm used to flying in helicopters, not planes."

Her hands steady on the yoke, Marly handled the aircraft like the expert she was. "Stick with me and I'll have you singing a different tune."

Pitbull shot a glance her way, his groin tightening despite the knot in his gut. He'd like to stick with Marly long enough to get to know her lithe body and the taste of her pink lips. The woman was sexy when she was all into her element of flying.

Pitbull wished he could enjoy the view more. And he might if he could relax, like she said, and enjoy the ride. But this wasn't Pitbull's preferred method of transport. It would take a whole lot more time in the craft for him to get even remotely comfortable. In the meantime, he'd suffer through, for the sake of the team.

MARLY ALMOST FELT sorry for Pitbull. Once she was over five hundred feet in the air, she shot a glance his way.

The man was as tense as a drawn bow-string. His knuckles were white where they curled around the armrest, and he stared through the front windshield unblinkingly.

She couldn't talk him down from his panic. She'd already tried. The best she could do was to land the plane safely and smoothly.

Marly had to admit Pitbull had been the one to catch her eye among the navy SEAL team members. His hard-packed body, square jaw and intense expression made her heart flutter, an occurrence she hadn't experienced in her twenty-nine years. Until she'd met the SEAL team and Pitbull.

Knowing he had a deep fear of fixed-wing aircraft didn't diminish his attraction in the least. It actually increased it in Marly's eyes. It proved he wasn't perfect, like she'd origi-nally thought. After her first encounter with the team, she'd read up on the elite units of navy SEALs and what it took to become one. And wow! This man sitting beside her had braved some of the worst conditions and treatment, muscled through and had become one of America's best.

From what she'd learned from others among the team, they'd deployed multiple times to the Middle East, Africa and other places around the world on deadly missions. Pitbull couldn't be afraid of much, if he strode headlong into danger.

Marly had waded into dangerous situations on more than one occasion and been scared she wouldn't emerge alive. But somehow, she had. Many times she'd considered moving back to the States and setting up a charter service there, but her mother still worked in the small villages of Africa, helping serve the poor and sick. Until her mother left Africa, she figured she might as well stay. Marly didn't have friends or family in Virginia, where she was born. Why go back?

She glanced over at the man in the seat beside her. Perhaps if she had someone to go home to…

Not that Pitbull was that someone. Marly had grown up independent, running wild in the villages where her mother and father had worked. She wasn't sure she'd be able to handle a full-time relationship. Freedom was everything to her.

And sometimes, with that freedom came loneliness.

Time passed. Marly made the scheduled stop to refuel at a small airfield halfway to their destination in northern Kenya. Her landing was so soft, she could have been kissing the ground. It didn't matter—Pitbull had a death grip on the armrest anyway.

The men clambered out, made their visit to the latrine and hurried back as the attendant completed the refueling. Pitbull offered to let someone else sit in the copilot's seat, but there were no takers.

Marly hid a smile. She didn't want someone else riding shotgun. She liked the view inside the cockpit.

Her takeoff was a little less graceful as she hit a couple pockets of air that tipped the wings slightly, making the plane wobble on the ascent. Marly sighed. She couldn't win every time.

Over the next hour, the color slowly returned to Pitbull's knuckles as he loosened his grip on the armrest.

Marly glanced at the savanna ahead and

spotted some of Africa's finest wildlife. She turned her head toward the rear of the plane. "If you look out to the southwest, you'll see herds of water buffalo and zebras."

The men in the seats behind her leaned forward and peered through the cabin windows.

Pitbull sat forward and craned his neck, scanning the land below.

"If you look carefully, I'll bet you can see a pride of lions lurking nearby." Marly tipped the nose of the plane downward.

Pitbull sat back, his grip tightening again on the armrest. "What are you doing?" he said, his voice clipped, his lips pulled back into a tight line.

"It's okay," Marly said. "I'm getting a little lower so you can see the animals."

"Isn't that what the safari is for?" Pitbull asked.

"Yes, but you can't see the vastness of the herd from the ground like you can from the air."

Buck laid a hand on Pitbull's shoulder. "Stop worrying and start drinking in this amazing view."

Pitbull closed his eyes briefly, sucked in a deep breath and let it out before nodding and reopening his eyes. "You're right. I need to stop worrying. This plane will get us there."

"And the excellent pilot," Buck added.

Marly shot a grateful smile over her shoulder. "Thanks for the vote of confidence."

And then, without warning, the engine sputtered, coughed and died.

Marly set the plane altitude for the best glide speed and turned her focus to the control panel. Her experience and training kicked in.

"What's happening?" Pitbull's voice said into her ear.

She didn't respond, needing every second of her attention on safely landing the disabled plane. Because they were so low already, Marly mentally went through an abbreviated emergency checklist and lowered the landing gear, all while scanning the surroundings for a suitable place to land.

Marly keyed her mic. "Mayday, mayday, mayday."

"Holy hell," Pitbull whispered beside her.

She'd promised to keep him safe on this flight, probably jinxing them all in the process. "Bravo-bravo-niner-eight-niner, experiencing engine failure. Bearing down on the savanna twenty miles north of the All Things Wild Safari & Resort, seven souls on board."

The air traffic controller acknowledged her distress call and offered to send a rescue crew to the location of their transponder.

Marly eased back on the yoke, trading airspeed for altitude, aiming the plane in the direction of the longest, flattest spot on the huge field. Unfortunately, it was occupied by a herd of zebras and water buffalos.

She couldn't take her gaze off the ground ahead, so she raised her voice loud enough that the men in the rear could hear. "Gentlemen, brace yourselves for a rough landing."

Chapter Two

When the engine cut out, Pitbull's heart slammed against his ribs and pulsed through his veins until Marly gave the warning to brace for landing. Then, as with all dangerous assignments, he drew into himself and focused on the mission.

In this case, it was to survive and get everyone out of what would surely be burning wreckage, if they were lucky enough to be alive upon landing.

"Move, damn you," Marly muttered into the mic, her concentration on the zebras trotting across the field in front of the descending plane. "Move."

The closer the plane grew to the herd, the faster they ran.

Pitbull leaned forward, his breath lodged in his throat, counting the seconds until they ran over the black-and-white-striped creatures. Just when he thought they'd hit one of the animals with the landing gear, the herd split, shooting out to each side of the aircraft and far enough away that the wings didn't touch them.

The plane floated toward the earth, slowing, slowing, slowing...

A horn sounded.

"What's that?" Pitbull demanded, searching the interior and exterior of the plane.

"Stall warning. Relax," Marly said through gritted teeth. "I've got this." She set the plane down on the savanna, the wheels kissing the earth. Once the nose wheel was down, they bounced across the uneven terrain.

By the time the plane came to a halt, Pitbull was convinced he'd rattled away every tooth in his mouth. But they were alive, the plane was intact and no fire ensued. He let go of the breath he'd been holding and leaned back in his seat.

"Wow, Marly," Buck said from the rear. "That was amazing."

Marly sat for a moment, staring at the departing herds, her lips pressed tightly together. Then she nodded, as if pulling herself back to the present, and peeled her fingers from the yoke. She turned with a tight smile and faced the men in the back. "Well, you wanted a safari. I didn't see any reason to wait." She held up her hand. "Don't worry. I won't charge you extra for the exciting landing."

Harm shook his head. "What happened?"

"I don't know, but I'm going to find out." She pushed out of her seat and waded through the team to the door. Once she'd lowered the steps, she hurried to the ground and around to the engine compartment.

The team piled out, leaving Pitbull to exit the aircraft last.

He fought the urge to drop to his knees and kiss the ground. If his legs were a little wobbly, he couldn't help it. Though Marly had done an excellent job landing the plane among a herd of zebras, she could just as easily have crashed and killed every last one of them.

The water buffalo and zebras stopped running and went back to grazing, as though it were an everyday occurrence to be disturbed by landing airplanes.

Pitbull trailed behind the others as they followed Marly.

"Need a hand?" T-Mac asked.

Marly lifted the lid to the engine compartment. "Know anything about airplanes?"

T-Mac shrugged. "No, but I'm handy with a variety of engines and computer issues."

"You're welcome to look over my shoulder." Marly opened the luggage compartment and started tossing backpacks and duffel bags to the ground. "I have a ladder in here somewhere." Once she'd dumped everything else out of the way, she said, "There it is." She yanked a small ladder out and stood it beside the plane. "Unlike all of you, I'm not six feet tall." She climbed up and leaned over the engine.

"I've had engines quit in my car before due to fuel pump issues," T-Mac offered.

"The fuel pump was replaced during the last annual maintenance on this plane," Marly said. "But that doesn't mean it didn't go bad since then." She looked down at Pitbull. "There's a tool bag behind the back seat inside the plane. Could you get it for me?"

Pitbull nodded and hurried to comply. When he returned, Marly and T-Mac had their heads together, staring into the engine.

A flush of heat washed over Pitbull. He fought the urge to insinuate himself between the two. Hell, they were within kissing distance. Instead, Pitbull cleared his throat and shoved the tool kit between Marly and T-Mac. "Perhaps this will help."

T-Mac leaned back.

Marly didn't take the bag. Instead, she stared into the engine. "Could you hand me a crescent wrench, please?"

Pitbull bit back a retort, unzipped the bag and gave her what she asked for.

She reached into the engine with the wrench and jerked back her hand. "Damn. You'd think it would have cooled down by now."

"Here, let me see." T-Mac took her arm and inspected the inside of her wrist.

"I'll be all right." Marly tugged her hand free and bent over the engine again. A few minutes later, she pulled out a part, shaking her head. "Like you said, it's the fuel pump. Looks like it burned up." She handed him the part and leaned over the engine. "Thankfully, it's the only thing burned up. A new part and this plane will be in the air again." She straightened and grimaced. "It'll be a rough takeoff, but I've been in worse places."

"Speaking of being in worse places." Harm

stepped up beside Pitbull. "How are we getting out of here?"

"I put in a call to the ATC. He said he'd send out a rescue crew." Marly closed the engine compartment and started to step down from the ladder.

Pitbull reached out and took her hand to steady her. When she laid hers in his, he felt the tingle of electricity race up his arm and spread across his chest. He didn't have time to analyze the feeling before she slipped on the last rung of the latter and pitched forward, slamming into his chest.

Pitbull went down, landing hard on his back, but cushioning Marly's fall. She landed on his chest, her hands on the ground on either side of his arms.

"Sorry," she said and scrambled to get off him. In the process, she kneed him in the groin.

Pain shot through him, wiping out the heat of the electricity her touch had generated. Pitbull doubled up, swallowing hard on the groan rising up his throat.

"I'm sorry," Marly repeated. As she straightened and brushed the dirt off her hands, her cheeks flamed red. She held out her hand to Pitbull.

"I'm all right," he said through clenched teeth, waving away her efforts. For a long moment, he lay still, willing the pain to go away.

"Well, damn." Marly knelt beside him and started to reach for the parts still pulsing with pain. "Is there anything I can do to help?"

He let go of his package and grabbed her wrist to keep her from touching him down there. Hell, if she didn't leave his parts alone, it wouldn't be long before he embarrassed himself in an entirely different way, pain be damned.

Buck laughed out loud. "Can't believe you let a girl clock your nads, dude." He nodded to Big Jake. "You get one side, I'll get the other."

"I'll get up when I'm ready," Pitbull insisted.

"You're ready," Big Jake announced. With one of his buddies on either side of him, Pitbull was brought to his feet. Not that he was quite ready. He did his best to stand up straight, thankful the pain faded with each breath.

Marly stared across the grassy plains, the color still high in her cheeks. "Shouldn't be too long. The ATC would have called someone close to our location. We never know what we're going to get." She entered the plane and walked from front to rear.

"Well, we might as well enjoy being this up close and personal with the African natives." Diesel walked past the tip of a wing and stared out over the savanna. "I don't think I've actually seen a water buffalo or zebra from this close."

"You're not as close as you'll be on the safari." Marly pulled a rag out of her back pocket and wiped the grease off her fingers.

"May I?" Pitbull held out his hand for the rag.

Marly's brows drew together, and she ran her gaze over him as she handed him the towel.

His lips quirked upward. "Don't be so suspicious." He leaned toward her and wiped a smudge of grease from her jaw. "You missed a spot."

Her cheeks blossomed with color. "Thank you." She swiped the rag from his hands and stuffed it back into her pocket before turning to the others. "We're not too far from the resort. If we're lucky, we won't have to wait more than an hour before someone shows up to take us there."

"An hour?" Buck asked.

Marly shrugged. "You never know who or how they will arrive. I'm assuming in a ground vehicle."

"I'd give my left nut for a whirly bird," Pitbull muttered. "We wouldn't be in this situation if we'd started out in a helicopter."

Marly rounded on Pitbull, eyes blazing, and jabbed her finger into Pitbull's chest. "If we'd been in a helicopter and the fuel pump went out, those vultures would be picking our bones clean." She redirected her pointer finger to a flock of vultures riding the air currents several hundred yards away.

Pitbull held up his hands. "Okay, okay. You made your point."

"Damn right I did. I'd like to see your helicopter pilots land as smoothly without an engine."

Buck draped an arm over Marly's shoulders. "You were awesome." He shot a glare at Pitbull. "We're alive, aren't we?"

Pitbull returned his buddy's glare and then nodded, letting the tension seep out of his body. "You're right." He held out his hand to Marly. "You did great landing the plane."

She stared at it for a moment, but didn't take it.

Pitbull dropped his arm, somewhat relieved. The last time she'd touched him with her hand, electricity had ricocheted throughout his body. He'd be better off enforcing a hands-off policy with Marly.

"I thought we were going to have zebra stew for dinner, as close as we came to landing on them," Harm said. "How did you know they'd get out of the way in time?"

Marly ducked from beneath Buck's arm. "I didn't. That was pure luck. Landing without damaging the plane..." She straightened her shoulders and flung back her ponytail. "That was all me."

It was true—Pitbull had been in the co-pilot's seat the whole way down. Marly had done a hell of a job piloting the craft to the ground among a herd of zebras and on bumpy terrain. "I guess I should thank you. But all I can think about is the fact you broke your promise."

She shook her head. "No I didn't."

"You said you wouldn't crash the plane," he told her.

"No, I said I wouldn't pass out while flying." She winked. "Those are two completely different things. And I didn't crash the plane."

Pitbull waved his hand toward the aircraft. "It's not flying."

She crossed her arms over her chest. "But it will, once I get the replacement part."

"How soon will that be?" Pitbull panned the surrounding savanna. "There aren't any aviation superstores anywhere nearby. And you can't seriously think you can take off on this field."

"I'm sure I can get a replacement part within a couple of days. And when I can find a smooth enough stretch, long enough to build up some speed, I can get this bird off the ground." She shook her head, a disgusted look on her face. "What do you know about avionics, anyway?"

Marly walked several yards away and stood staring at the animals in the distance, her back to the men. The band holding her ponytail had slipped loose. Strands of silky, sandy-blond hair caught in the breeze.

Pitbull couldn't tear his gaze off her slim,

athletic figure encased in the form-hugging flight suit.

Buck leaned close to his friend and whispered, "You're a knucklehead."

"What's your point?" Pitbull snapped back, too engaged in his view of Marly to care what Buck had to say.

"She landed the plane," Buck said.

T-Mac added, "That's right. We're alive. You should be down on your knees, groveling at her feet."

His teammates were right. What was it about Marly that got Pitbull all fired up? She was smart and sexy and knew her way around her airplane. Why couldn't he leave her alone?

She turned, a smile on her face.

That smile hit him square in the chest like a round from a .55-caliber machine gun. He almost staggered back a few steps with the impact.

"Here comes our rescue team." Marly pointed to a cloud of dust rising from the grass, heading straight for them.

The men gathered around Marly, like cowboys circling their wagons.

"Are you sure that's our rescue team?" Pitbull asked.

"Who else would be out in the middle of nowhere?" Marly's brows dipped. "Seriously, the ATC had our coordinates from the transponder. They had to have passed them on to whoever they called."

"We've seen some of the welcoming committees here in Africa," Harm said, squinting at the oncoming vehicle.

"If you're worried, wait behind me." Marly unzipped her flight suit to reveal a pink bra beneath and a shoulder holster. She pulled out a nine-millimeter handgun.

The team all backed up several steps, every man raising his hands.

"Whoa there, Marly," Buck said. "Do you know how to use that thing?"

She glared at him. "Do you think I'd carry it if I didn't?"

Buck shrugged. "Some women do."

"I'd be a fool to fly around this country unarmed, now, wouldn't I?" She nodded toward the vehicle now visible through the cloud of dust. "Looks like a safari wagon."

"And it's not empty." Pitbull dove for his backpack, unearthed the M4A1 he'd stashed inside and quickly assembled the main parts.

"Hold your fire, Zippy," Marly said. "They

wouldn't come out without a contingent of armed men. The animals can cause enough damage, but the poachers and warring rebels are even more dangerous. Wait and see."

"If we wait too long, we could all be dead." Pitbull took up a position in the shadow of the airplane and lined up his sights with the driver of the oncoming truck.

"I'm with Pitbull." Harm reached for his backpack and pulled out a .45-caliber hand-gun.

The other four men did the same. Soon, everyone waiting at the plane was armed and ready for whatever was headed their way.

The big truck pulled to a lumbering stop several yards away from the plane.

A woman appeared out of the cloud of dust, wearing tall leather riding boots, khaki slacks tucked into the top of the boots and a matching khaki shirt, unbuttoned to reveal an ample amount of cleavage. She swept a wide-brimmed safari hat from her head and shook out auburn curls. "We're here to help."

Buck let out a long, low whistle. "Wow."

She was followed by three dark-skinned men dressed in khaki uniforms and carrying machine guns.

Pitbull aimed for the first one, keeping all three in his peripheral vision. If any one of them made a move, he'd take them down.

"Hey, don't shoot!" a sultry voice called out. "We're really here to help."

Chapter Three

Marly shoved her pistol back into the holster beneath her flight suit and stepped forward, holding out her hand to the woman who came to a halt in front of her. "Marly Simpson. I'm the pilot. You got here fast."

The other woman was shorter, curvier and stunningly beautiful. Next to her, Marly felt like the ugly stepsister to Cinderella. She shoved aside the thought and shook the woman's hand.

"Talia Montclair. Nice to meet you." She shook Marly's hand with a firm grip and turned to the others. "I'm from All Things Wild Safari & Resort. We got a call from the local police to come pick up the passengers and crew from an aircraft since it went down closest to our operations." She stared around at the others. "Anyone badly hurt? I'm also a trained paramedic."

Buck lifted his hand.

Talia's brows rose. "What's the nature of your injury?"

He pressed the hand to his chest. "You just stole my heart."

Talia planted her hands on her hips, her lips quirking on the corners. "Seriously, was anyone injured in the landing?"

"No." Pitbull stepped out from the shadows and lowered his rifle. "Thanks to our pilot." He glanced at Marly with a slight nod and then held out his hand to Talia. "Percy Taylor."

Marly chuckled softly. Finally, the man acknowledged her skill in landing the plane. But did he have to hold Talia's grip for so long?

"That's his real name, but we call him Pitbull." Buck bumped Pitbull out of the way and held out his hand to the safari representative. "Graham Buckner. But you can call me Buck."

Talia grinned. "Percy, Graham, nice to meet you." She faced the other four men. "I'm assuming the rest of you are Dalton, Harmon, Trace and Jake?" Her smile spread wider.

They nodded as one.

"Good." She clapped her hands together. "My safari adventurers. And I see you couldn't wait to get started and decided to land in the middle of our first stop for tomorrow." She waved her hand toward the herd. "Welcome to Kenya. Like what you see so far?"

Marly's lips thinned. For the most part, the men weren't looking at the herds of wild animals. Instead, they were drooling over their safari guide, Talia.

Heat built in Marly's gut. And not the good lusty kind. More the jealous, burning, I-can't-compete-with-that kind. She glanced down at her flight suit that did little to disguise her lack of a voluptuous figure. She was too tall and lanky to be considered feminine. Not that it had bothered her. Until now.

She dared a glance at Pitbull. She was pleased to see he wasn't looking at Talia.

Instead, his gaze was on Talia's guards.

Talia must have noticed their regard. "Don't let my men scare you. We have to come armed." She nodded toward the SEALs' weapons. "And I'm glad to see you brought your own firepower. We run into all kinds of four-and two-legged aggressors out here. It pays to be prepared." Talia glanced toward the plane, her eyes narrowing. "Speaking of which, we might want to push the plane into the tree line."

Marly glanced around the open field, searching for a stand of trees large enough to park the plane beneath. "The engine isn't working."

Talia smiled. "I'm sure you can get some old-fashioned brawn to help get it where you want it to go. I wouldn't leave it out in the open. You never know what might happen if it's left alone."

Familiar with the nature of the inhabitants of the savannas and jungles of Africa, Marly agreed. Gangs of miscreants, poachers and rebels would have the plane stripped of anything salvageable in no time.

She located a copse of trees three hundred yards to her south. "If we could get it to that stand of trees, I'd feel better about leaving it."

Pitbull stepped forward. "Let us handle it."

The six SEALs and the three guards positioned themselves around the aircraft at Marly's direction and began pushing the plane across the bumpy terrain and toward the trees.

Talia followed in the truck.

Once they had the plane positioned between the trees, Talia hauled out a large bundle from the back of the truck and dropped it on the ground. "You can use this camouflage netting to conceal the plane. Trust me, I wouldn't want anyone to find it. We've had some near misses with a local rebel group. The cowards try to get our people alone. Then they attack and steal whatever they might sell on the black market. They'd steal this plane piece by piece if they found it."

"Should I stay with the plane until the part comes?" Marly asked.

"I think it will be okay as long as you conceal it well enough."

"Great," Marly said, grabbing a corner of the netting.

The others took up the other ends and dragged the net over the nose and wings, and finally over the tail.

When they had secured the ends to the ground using sticks and rocks, Marly stood back and examined the effect. From a distance, it would blend into the shadows of the trees.

Talia waved toward the truck. "We can fit

two inside—me and one other—and the rest in the back. I'll let you figure out who goes where."

Pitbull hurried to the front of the vehicle and opened the passenger seat. "Marly," he barked like a command.

Marly, unused to having men open doors for her, glanced toward the rear of the truck. "I can ride in the back. You guys are the clients."

"Don't be ridiculous." Buck hooked her arm, marched her to the passenger side and handed her off to Pitbull. "You'll ride up front. We're used to eating dust."

"So am I," Marly argued.

Pitbull leaned close and whispered in her ear, "Are you always this disagreeable?"

She frowned at him. "Sometimes I'm even more so."

Pitbull gripped her around the waist and lifted her up to the seat, ending the argument.

Marly sat down hard, shocked that he'd manhandled her so easily. She'd always considered herself to be too big to be girly. But Pitbull had just proven he was strong enough to sweep this independent, no-nonsense woman off her feet.

Her heart fluttered and her cheeks heated.

Where his hands had clenched around her waist still tingled with awareness. She clamped her mouth shut and stared forward, refusing to look back at the man who'd set her blood speeding through her veins and pooling low in her belly.

What was wrong with her? This man was a US Navy SEAL. He probably had a woman in every port. Even if he didn't, his job had him traveling the world at the drop of a hat. Nothing could ever come of a relationship with such a man.

Nothing.

PITBULL DIDN'T REGRET ending the argument with Marly by lifting her into the truck. He did regret the lingering electrical current running up his arms and down to his groin. *Focus, man. Focus.*

They were in Kenya for only a week. *Let's go on a safari,* his teammates had said. *It'll be fun,* they'd assured him. Nothing was fun about the raging lust spinning through his body for the woman he'd just touched, not when he knew it wouldn't go anywhere. He wouldn't be able to act on it. Thankfully, Marly would be gone as soon as she had her fuel pump. Hopefully that would be by the end of the day. Then he could concentrate on having a good time seeing all the animals and enjoying the resort. And maybe they could convince the 160th to send a helicopter out to retrieve them. They could call it a training mission to extricate military personnel from a hostile environment.

He climbed into the back of the truck with the other members of his team and held on tight. The trip to the resort was across the savanna and into a forest. An hour later, they pulled up to a large, rambling house made of wood and stone. The house was surrounded by smaller huts with a similar wood-and-stone design—individual cottages Pitbull guessed were options for their guests.

Talia parked the truck in front of the main house and climbed down.

"I have each of you in your own bungalow, but meals will be in the main house dining room," Talia said. "Breakfast and lunch are casual. Dinner is formal. Please dress accordingly. Follow me, if you will." She entered the house, leaving the door open behind her for them to follow.

The main house had a grand entrance with

staircases on each side curving up to the second floor. Shiny mahogany handrails and furniture gave the rooms elegance in a rugged land of wild animals and dangerous people.

"The dining room is to your left. Normally I rent out the guest rooms, but they are unoccupied at the present time. I thought you would prefer your own bungalows while you are with us at All Things Wild Resort. You're welcome to take advantage of the living areas and the sitting room on the main floor. At the back of the house is a game room with a pool table and a bar. I'll leave you to explore for yourself while I get Miss Simpson situated and gather the keys to your bungalows."

"I'm up for a round of pool." T-Mac started for the rear of the house. "Anyone else?"

Buck pushed past the others and followed T-Mac. "Count me in."

"I could go for a beer," Harm said.

"Me, too," Diesel agreed. "Maybe two."

"You're welcome to the beer, wine and the liquor cabinet. It's all included in the price of the week," Talia informed them.

Big Jake laughed. "You might regret telling them that."

"No worries. We have a well-equipped bar,

and the wines are from local vineyards." Talia motioned for Marly to follow her. "I have a satellite phone in the study, if you'd like to call someone about fixing your plane."

"Thank you." Marly followed Talia into a beautifully appointed study. The walls were lined with built-in bookshelves. A massive mahogany desk graced one end of the room. The room had a masculine scent of books and wood.

Talia crossed to the desk and lifted a portable satellite phone. She handed the device to Marly and then turned to a computer monitor, bringing up a browser. "Help yourself to the internet. We do most of our communications via satellite. Unfortunately, we're too remote for most cable or electric companies to keep up with those pesky lines."

Marly thanked Talia, sat down at the computer and pulled up an internet browser to locate a replacement for the fuel pump. An hour later, she had a man on the phone with her answer. Not the one she wanted to hear, however.

"Five days?" Marly shook her head, despite that the guy on the other end of the communication couldn't actually see her face as she spoke. "You can't get it to me any sooner?"

The man answered, "It's the best I can do. Take it or leave it."

Marly drew in a deep breath and let it go. "I'll take it. Thank you."

She stood and stretched. What now? She hadn't come prepared to be here for almost a week.

Talia poked her head through the open door of the study. "Find your part?"

Marly nodded and grimaced.

"Let me guess." Talia tipped her head to the side. "It'll be a week before they can get it to you."

Marly laughed. "You know how things work in these parts, I take it."

"Yes, indeed." Talia crossed her arms over her ample chest and leaned against the door frame. "The kitchen stove quit working once when I had the resort booked solid. It took over a month to get a replacement. My chef and I had to cook everything on the outdoor grill, rain or shine. We were not amused."

"Thankfully, it'll only take five days, not a month. But I didn't come prepared to stay overnight, much less five days."

"No worries. I can loan you clothes to last you, and we have extra toiletries for guests who've forgotten items." Talia touched her arm. "I can even cut you a deal on a room for the five days, since we're not full at this time."

"Thank you for the room offer." Marly bit her bottom lip. "Though I'm not sure your clothes will fit."

Talia ran her glance from Marly's head to her toes. "You're taller, so the full-length pants won't fit, but I have some formal dresses that will be ankle-length on you and shorts and capris you might fit into. We'll make it work."

"Dresses?" Marly cringed inwardly. "I haven't worn a dress since I was in grade school."

Talia's brows rose. "Darling, you'll have to around here, if you want dinner." She spun toward the door. "And I'll bet you have some great legs hiding under that flight suit. Follow me. You'll be staying in one of the upstairs suites inside the house. And I'll get you fixed up with clothes. If not from my wardrobe, well, people have left articles of clothing over the years. They've come in handy when luggage doesn't arrive with the guests."

Marly swallowed her groan. She liked her *own* clothes. They fit her and she felt like herself in them. *Beggars can't be choosers*, she reminded herself. She just hoped the tops Talia offered didn't hang on her chest, making her appear to be an underdeveloped teenager.

Again. Beggars can't be choosers.

TALIA HAD SHOWN Pitbull and the other members of his team to their individual bungalows while Marly made her calls to locate the spare part she needed to get her plane back up in the air.

Pitbull welcomed the time away from Marly. Since they'd left that morning, he couldn't get his mind off the feisty pilot. After their last mission, he hadn't expected to see her ever again. Even then, he'd felt that spark of something, if not between them, then at least on his side. He didn't much care for women who wore a lot of makeup or ratted their hair to achieve bigger, brassier hairstyles. He liked that Marly was natural and that she didn't apologize for it.

He tossed his backpack on the bed, tugged his T-shirt off and headed for the shower. After riding in the back of the old truck, he felt as if he had an inch of dust coating his body and filling all the crevices.

Nothing a little soap and water won't cure.

If only soap and water could wash Marly out of his head.

He turned the shower to a cool setting and stepped beneath the spray. As he lathered his body, running his hands over his skin, his thoughts drifted back to Marly and that damned flight suit. He wondered what it would be like to undress her body from that all-enveloping garment, starting at the zipper and working his way down. The glimpse of her hot-pink bra had only left him wanting to know more. Such as, did she have matching hot-pink panties?

His groin tightened and his shaft swelled at the image in his mind. She'd be appalled at his lusty thoughts, but he couldn't seem to stop them. At that moment, he wondered how her long legs would feel wrapped around his waist as he drove into her.

Pitbull reached behind him, turning the water to an even cooler temperature. He didn't need to show up at dinner and embarrass himself. The guys would rib him endlessly.

After rinsing the soap from his hair, face and body, he turned off the shower, stepped out of the tub and toweled dry with one of the huge luxury towels provided.

As a navy SEAL, he wasn't used to lavishness. Three squares and a bunk were all he'd come to hope for, and sometimes he went without. Having a shower at all was always a blessing. He pressed the towel to his nose and sniffed the light floral fragrance. Again, he thought of Marly and how that towel would wrap around her slender body twice.

He flung the towel over the curtain rod, pulled his razor out of his shaving kit and scraped three days' worth of beard from his chin. With a clean body and a smooth chin, he strode into the bedroom naked. Talia had said dinner was formal. He dug inside his backpack for his best white long-sleeved, button-down shirt and his only pair of dark trousers. He didn't have a suit jacket, but he could at least dress nicely for dinner.

The men had been warned that they needed at least one dressier outfit for dinners during their stay at the resort. Pitbull would have preferred to show up in his jeans and a T-shirt, but he had to respect the proprietress's rules. He shook his trousers and shirt, hoping to knock the wrinkles out. When that didn't work, he searched the small bungalow and found an ironing board. Great. Just what he wanted to do on vacation at a safari resort.

Pride forced him to pull the board and iron out. In less than ten minutes, he had the wrinkles smoothed. While the garments were still warm, Pitbull slipped into them and pulled on socks and shoes. He found the necktie he'd picked up at the Post Exchange on Camp Lemonnier, looped it over his neck and knotted it expertly. He might not have grown up in the best neighborhood, but his mother had taught him how to knot a tie for church.

He smiled at her memory. The woman had worked hard all her life, only to die of breast cancer when Pitbull had been in BUD/S training. She'd insisted he not come home for her funeral, knowing how difficult the training was and how much harder it would be to have to start over.

He still regretted not being with his mother at her bedside until her last breath. His parents had always been there for him and believed in him. They always told him that he could accomplish anything he set his mind to.

Except save his mother.

As an only child, he'd felt the burden of

guilt for not being there for her when she'd needed him most.

His father had been there, comforting her as she left life and, as he'd said, joined the angels.

Pitbull had never been sure of angels and religion, but he'd experienced days in battle when nothing but a miracle could have saved them, and then it had. He liked to think his mother had been watching over him.

His father was still alive, living in Virginia, still a little lost without his wife. He'd been heartbroken by the loss and hadn't dated or dared to love another woman since. Pitbull visited him as much as possible when he was Stateside in Little Creek, Virginia.

Having witnessed his father's heartache, Pitbull had been hesitant to get that involved with any woman for more than a date or two. He didn't want love someone he might lose, and suffer the way his father had.

This thing he was feeling about Marly was nothing more than insta-lust. It would fade and she'd be out of his life when they left Africa.

He ran a comb through his hair, smoothing it into place. The longer he took to get ready, the more jittery he became. Dressed thirty minutes early, he had nothing else to do but wait. Hell, he might as well wait outside.

He found himself anxious to see Marly again. How could that be? He barely knew the woman.

Chapter Four

Pitbull stepped out of his bungalow and noted Buck standing outside his. He gave the other man a slight lift of his chin and sauntered over to join him.

Buck wore a black button-down shirt and black trousers with a red necktie. He tugged at the tie. "Damned things are like a noose. Whoever invented them was either masochistic or sadistic."

Pitbull nodded. "I don't understand dressing in formal clothing for dinner. What's wrong with jeans?"

"Women." Buck shrugged and tipped his head toward the darkening shadows in the nearby trees. "Did you hear the hyenas laughing?"

His lips quivering in laughter, Pitbull shot back, "They think we look funny, too?"

With a snort, Buck started toward the main house. "I guess early is better than late to a formal dinner."

Pitbull glanced around. "Wonder if the others are ready."

"They were the last ones at the pool table and are running late. They'll find us soon enough," Buck responded.

As they neared the front entrance to the house, the sun was setting in a radiant wash of orange, red, mauve and finally blues and purples. The gap between the trees gave them just enough of the spectacle to make them stop and stare for a long moment.

The front door opened behind them.

"Gentlemen, won't you come into the study for a drink before dinner?" Talia stood in the doorway, dressed in a long gown that hugged every curve of her body like a second skin. The neckline was low, dipping past her breasts, but not quite down to her belly button. The woman was well endowed, and gravity hadn't yet made its claim there.

"Now I can see why formal dinners can be a draw," Buck said beneath his breath as he followed Talia inside. Louder he said, "Talia, you look amazing."

"Why, thank you." Talia stopped in the foyer and turned a smile toward Buck, her lips spreading across her expertly made-up face. "Wait until you see Marly. I got to experiment with clothes and makeup. I barely recognized her."

Pitbull's brows drew together. He hoped Talia hadn't painted Marly's smooth, natural complexion with a ton of makeup. He liked Marly's fresh face and naturally pink lips.

"Where is she?" Buck asked, craning his neck to see around Talia.

"She was combing her hair when I left her. Hopefully she won't be much longer." Her glance shifted from the men in the entryway to the sweeping staircases.

A figure moved toward the landing and paused at the top.

Pitbull's breath caught in his chest. He stared up at the woman standing there. She had on a sapphire-blue dress that hugged her body like she was born in it. The top crisscrossed her breasts and rounded the back of her neck in soft, iridescent folds. The skirt clung to her waist, hips and thighs, falling to the tops of her ankles, shimmering with every move and exposing a hint of her tight calves. Rhinestone-studded, low-heeled sandals completed her outfit, emphasizing her delicate feet.

With one hand on the rail, she descended the stairs, her head held high, sandy-blond tresses pulled up in a stylishly messy bun with strands falling down around her cheeks. Her gaze caught his, holding it all the way down.

Without realizing he'd moved, Pitbull found himself at the base of the stairs, his hand resting on the rail, his foot on the first riser.

A low whistle sounded next to him. "Is that our Marly?" Buck asked in a hushed tone.

Marly gave a lopsided grin. "It's me," she said and laughed.

When Buck held out his hand to her, Pitbull brushed it aside and reached out to take hers for himself.

Marly laid her fingers in his palm and shook her head. "You act as if you're staring at a unicorn." She wiggled her fingers in front of his face. "For that matter, you might as well be staring at a unicorn. When I leave here, you'll never see me in a dress again."

"Oh, Marly, darling, you look fabulous." Talia joined them and gave Marly a hug. "I knew that color would suit you perfectly."

Talia stood back, admiring Marly's transformation. "Don't you boys agree?"

"You look nice," Pitbull said. "I almost didn't recognize you."

"Beautiful, sweetheart." Buck leaned in and bussed Marly's cheek.

Her face flamed with color. "It's just a dress. A borrowed one at that."

"But you wear it so well," Talia insisted. "I have another dress that will be just as spectacular on you for tomorrow night."

"No." Marly held up her hand. "I can wear this one every night. You don't have to dress me in something different every evening."

"I insist," Talia said. "I don't often have lovely ladies visiting. It would be my pleasure. And you wouldn't want to deprive me of the fun, would you?"

Marly bit on her bottom lip and studied the other woman.

Pitbull could tell she was debating what she wanted to say to her hostess.

Finally Marly sighed. "I don't mind at all. If you want to dress me like a doll, I won't stop you. But I draw the line at corsets. I don't do corsets."

Talia laughed. "I'll remember that."

The front door opened, and the other four members of Pitbull's team entered. They gathered around Marly, congratulating her on her amazing transformation.

"You look like an entirely different woman," Harm commented.

She laughed out loud and then frowned. "No matter what I'm wearing, I'm still the same old Marly. And, for the record, I'd rather wear my flight suit and hiking boots than a dress and heels any day."

Talia raised her arms, urging the crowd of people toward another door. "If Miss Simpson and you men are ready, we can go into the dining room to be served."

Pitbull offered Marly his arm. As they entered the formal dining room, he leaned close to Marly and said, "You look amazing."

She ducked her head. "Thank you."

"But seriously," Pitbull added, "I prefer you in the flight suit and boots."

She shot a glance his way. "You don't like the dress?"

"Don't get me wrong, the dress suits you. But I like the pilot, Marly—the woman who likes to putter in airplane engines and get grease on her cheek."

She ducked her head again, color blooming in her face. "You do?" Glancing up, she caught his gaze. "Why?"

Before Pitbull could think of a response, Talia interrupted his thoughts.

"There are no assigned seats. You may sit wherever your heart desires." She pinned Marly and Pitbull with a stare and a half smile.

Was it a challenge? Pitbull didn't know, nor did he care. He was still working through how he would answer Marly's question without revealing too many of his internal thoughts.

He held out a chair for her and waited while she got situated. When he went to sit in the space beside her, he was outmaneuvered by Buck.

"Hey." He laid a hand on Buck's shoulder.

"You snooze, you lose, buddy." Buck grinned up at him. "Besides, I want to get to know this new, sexy Marly. She's *hot*."

By the time Pitbull turned to the seat on the other side of Marly, Big Jake had settled in.

When Pitbull glared at him, he frowned. "What? Do you want me to move or something?"

He wanted to say *Get the hell out of my seat*, but why? Marly wasn't his property. He had no more of a valid reason to sit beside her than any one of his teammates. They all wanted to be close to the beauty she'd transformed into. The only difference between him and them was they wanted her for what she'd become. Pitbull wanted Marly for the woman in the flight suit, not the one in the fancy blue dress.

He took the seat across the table from her and contented himself with staring at her as often as he liked.

The meal was excellent, served in seven courses. By the time dinner was over, Pitbull could swear he'd ground his back teeth into nubs. Who ate dinner over the space of two hours? The longest meal he'd ever had lasted maybe fifteen minutes, tops. In the military, you ate fast, not knowing when you'd be interrupted by enemy fire.

He wanted out of the suffocating pretentiousness of the house, out in the night where he could stretch his arms and legs, and remember what it meant to be free. At least there, the animals wouldn't give a damn which fork he used with the salad and which he used with dessert.

When the dessert was served, he jammed it

down his throat, pushed back from the table and half stood, ready to make a run for the exit.

"Mr. Taylor, are you up on the dangers of the African safari?" Talia asked.

He sat back down in the chair. For a long time, he didn't say anything. Finally, he nodded. "I know not to move around alone in the night and to make sure my weapon of choice will bring down a man or an elephant, whichever attacks me first."

Talia nodded. "You're right. The four-legged animals can get testy when you invade their space. They usually don't attack in this area, but we've had a rogue lion sneak in the past few nights and steal away a farm animal or, in the worst-case scenario, a child."

Marly's soft gasp could be heard around the table. "Did they find the child?"

Talia shook her head, her mouth turning downward at the corners. "Sadly, no."

Marly glanced down at her half-eaten cheesecake. "I'm sorry to hear that."

Talia forced a smile to her lips. "My goal wasn't to make for depressing dinner conversation. I just want you to be aware of the dangers lurking in the dark. Don't go out alone, and don't assume you're safe. The animals have learned humans can be easy targets." She placed her palms on the table and stood. "That said, please don't hesitate to enjoy the walled gardens behind the house. We've never had any big cats attempt to scale the walls."

When Talia had risen from the table, all of the men rose with her.

Pitbull pushed his chair up to the table. "On that note, I could use some fresh air."

"Please, make yourself at home," Talia said. "And you're welcome to play pool as late as you like, or have drinks at the bar. The house is well insulated, so the noise won't bother other guests."

Harm nodded toward T-Mac. "You and I have a game to win. We can't let Big Jake and Diesel claim the title."

Big Jake shook his head. "I'm out. I'd rather have a beer and watch." He tipped his head toward Buck. "Let Buck and Diesel clean your clocks."

Buck cracked his knuckles. "You won't have a chance against me and Diesel."

T-Mac laughed. "I've seen you play. You're all talk."

"Put your money where your mouth is," Buck said. "I've got a twenty saying we'll win."

"Make it thirty. I could use the extra cash in my pocket," T-Mac shot back.

"You ladies care to join us?" Harm asked Marly and Talia.

Talia smiled. "I'd love to."

Marly shook her head. "I'll pass. Sounds too intense for me. I've had my share of intensity for the day."

"Right." Harm nodded. "Landing a plane in the middle of a herd of water buffalos and zebras has to be a bit extreme." He shrugged. "If you get bored or lonely, join us anytime."

"Yeah." Buck winked. "We'll be up late wiping the floor with these guys."

The five men and Talia left the room, heading for the back of the house.

Pitbull rounded the table and stopped in front of Marly. "I could use some peace and quiet. How about you?"

"The garden sounds like the place to be. I don't know about you, but the guys can be overwhelming in large doses."

Pitbull nodded. "Yeah. I get that." He held out his arm.

Marly frowned but slipped her hand in the

crook of his elbow. "This is all so foreign to me. I grew up for the most part in small villages, running barefoot, wearing jeans and shorts." She plucked at the dress. "I'm not used to this kind of finery. I feel like a big fake."

Pitbull led her toward the exit and they emerged from the house into the garden, where exotic flowers and bushes and their softness surrounded them, along with the familiar fragrance of roses. They reminded him of his mother's rose garden.

"You wear that dress beautifully. But I get what you're saying. The only times I wear suits are for funerals and the odd covert operation. These danged ties are killer." He reached up and loosened the knot at his neck.

Marly chuckled beside him. "Here, let me." She turned to face him, reached up and pulled the knot free on the tie. "Better?" Her eyes sparkled with the reflection of the moonlight glinting in her irises. Her lips curled in a pretty smile, and it was beyond Pitbull's ability to resist her.

"Much." He pulled her against him.

Marly raised her hands to his chest, but didn't push back.

Pitbull lifted one hand to cup the back of her head. The other circled to the small of her back, pressing her hips against his. "I don't know if it's the moonlight, this garden or that dress, but right now all I want to do is kiss you."

Her fingers curled into his shirt and she stared up into his gaze. "You do?" Her voice wasn't much more than a whisper, her breath warm on his chin.

"Tell me to let go, and I will."

"PLEASE, DON'T." MARLY clung to the man, her knees more like wet noodles, incapable of holding her up.

He chuckled, his breath stirring the loose hairs around her face. "Don't what? Don't hold you like this?" He tightened his hand at the base of her back, pressing her body to his more firmly. "Or don't let go?"

She swept her tongue across her lips, afraid to voice what she wanted, but more afraid he'd take her silence as a rejection. "Don't let go." Marly leaned into him, reveling in the feel of his hard muscles beneath the crisp white shirt. She wanted to run her hands over his bare skin and inhale his masculine scent. He was intoxicating. If she didn't watch out, she'd be drunk with her lust. And then what?

Marly stilled her hands' roving. "You should know something about me." She had to say it. He might as well know.

Pitbull stared down into her eyes. "What's that?" He kissed her forehead, the tip of her nose and each cheek.

Marly closed her eyes, loving the feel of his lips against her skin. "I've been around men all my life, but I'm not well versed in the art of seduction. I've been too busy to have a love life. I don't know how to be feminine and girly. I've only been on a couple dates, and they were disasters." She opened her eyes and grimaced. "What I'm trying to say is, I hope you're not disappointed."

Pitbull lowered his head, taking her lips in a kiss that changed her world. Her insides exploded with sensations like she'd never felt before, sending electrical charges zipping through her veins and nerves. She couldn't recall a time she'd had so little control of her reactions to another human being.

Marly curled her hands around his neck, afraid that if she didn't hold on, she'd melt to the floor, every bone in her body liquefying at his touch.

When he traced the seam of her lips with his tongue, she opened to him on a soft gasp.

His tongue swept past her teeth to tangle with hers, caressing, sliding in and out, warm, wet and tasting of the strawberry cheesecake from their dessert.

Tentatively at first, she dared to meet his tongue with hers.

His arms tightened around her and he stepped closer, their bodies now touching from shoulders to thighs. The heat generated between them eclipsed that of the lingering savanna warmth.

Marly wanted to be even closer, but that could be accomplished only by being naked. She slipped her hands beneath the collar of his shirt, loving the feel of his skin and the sinewy muscles of his neck and shoulders.

Pitbull's hand at her back slipped beneath the edge of the low-back gown, sliding toward the rounded curve of her bottom.

She tensed, unused to a man caressing her naked skin. He slowed his descent and held true, his fingers massaging, tempting, relaxing her until she sighed and once again leaned into him.

When he finally lifted his head, he pressed his forehead to hers and removed his hand from beneath her dress. "You tempt me like no other."

Marly gave a shaky laugh, not quite sure how to respond. "Ditto," she said, wishing she could dream up something hot and sexy to say in return. Hell, she wasn't cut out for the mating rituals others were so much better at. Pitbull had to have been with a dozen women, all of whom likely had more experience in their little fingers than Marly had in her entire twenty-nine years of living.

"Hey." Pitbull tipped her chin up, forcing her to look into his eyes. The light from the moon shone down on his face, illuminating a concerned dent in his brow. "What's wrong?"

"I'm not like other women," she said tentatively.

He laughed. "How so?"

"I told you. I'm not experienced. I don't know how to make you…" She shrugged, her cheeks burning with embarrassment.

"How to make me want you? How to make me long for another kiss? How to make me want to toss you over my shoulder and take you to my cabin for the night?" he offered.

"Yes. That." She stared up at him, wishing she knew any of the skills required in flirting.

"Would it help to know I appreciate that you aren't like other women? That I'm so turned on right now, it's all I can do not to rip off your clothes and have you right here?" He set her away from him and ran a hand through his hair.

Her insides hummed with the lingering effects of his kiss and the words he'd just said. "You want me?"

He chuckled and pulled her close to him again. "You tell me."

This time she could feel the hard ridge beneath his trousers. Marly's eyes widened. If she had the courage, she'd reach out and touch it. Alas, she didn't know what was expected or considered acceptable on a first date. Yes, she'd dated. But not often enough to know all the rules and etiquette.

Not that this had been their first date. But it had been their first kiss. This romance thing was confusing. She drew in a deep breath to steady herself and let it go, glancing up at Pitbull. "Where do we go from here?" With all her heart, she wanted him to say *Back to my cabin*.

He cupped her cheeks and pressed a kiss to her forehead, then took a step backward, dropping his arms to his sides. "You'll go to your room, and I'll go to my cabin."

Marly frowned, disappointment like a knife in her gut. "Are you sure that's where you want to go?"

He shook his head. "Oh, hell no. But for now, it'll have to do." Pitbull jabbed a thumb to his chest and then pointed at her. "You and I are in two very different places in our lives. Not to mention, we're usually separated by an ocean. Whatever this is…nothing will come of it."

"So?" Marly took a step forward. He wanted her. He'd said so in no uncertain terms. "What's stopping us from being together now?"

Again he shoved his hand through his hair. "Marly, you're not the type of girl a man can make love to and leave. You deserve someone who will stick around and be there for you."

"What if I don't want that?" Okay, so she didn't know how to flirt. But she did know what she wanted.

Him.

"You said you don't know what you want," he pointed out.

"That's not what I said. I said I didn't have any experience in the lovemaking department." She stopped when she got so close, she could feel the heat of his body without touching him. "What if I want you to teach me what I need to know?"

Pitbull held up his hands. "If I were any other man, I'd take you up on it. But I can't do that."

"Why?" She laid her hand on his chest and flicked a button open on his shirt. She wanted him so badly, she threw caution to the wind, took a deep breath and dove in. "No strings attached. I won't expect you to fall in love with me or be there after you leave Africa." She forced a saucy smile, cocked her brow and challenged him with a direct stare. All the while she quaked inside.

"What do you have to lose?"

Chapter Five

Marly couldn't believe the words coming out of her own mouth. Was this the same woman who'd just admitted she didn't have experience in making love? She'd just handed him the proverbial key to her bedroom, giving him carte blanche, no strings attached. Holy hell! What was he waiting for?

He raised his hands to grip her arms. "You don't really want this."

Oh yes, she did. "No? In the short time since you met me, have you known me to say something I don't mean?" She flicked another button on his shirt.

His chest rose and fell on a deeply inhaled breath, and then he caught her wrist in his hand. "No. Not like this."

The wind left her sails and she stepped back, pulling free of his grasp, her entire body flushed with the warmth of embarrassment. "I'm sorry. I told you I wasn't good at this." She turned and walked several steps away. "You're right. We should go our separate ways and forget what just happened."

Most likely, Pitbull wouldn't even think about the fiery kiss ever again, unless he was telling the story about the bush pilot who'd given a pathetic woman's imitation of seduction. His teammates would get a great laugh out of that one.

"Marly." Pitbull's deep voice sounded directly behind her, and he reached out to touch her shoulder.

She shook it off and took another step away from him. "Really, you should go play pool with your friends, or go back to your cabin. Alone."

"I'm not leaving until you're safely inside the house."

"Talia said they never had wild animals in the walled garden." She waved toward the ten-foot-high brick-and-stucco wall. "I'll be fine."

Pitbull made no move to leave.

Marly spun on the high-heeled sandals Talia had loaned her and nearly fell. Gathering as much dignity as she could after wobbling on her feet, she lifted her chin and said, "Please, just go." She turned away and started for the rose arbor.

A low, throaty growl rumbled in the shadows, bringing her to a grinding stop.

Marly froze, her heart skipping several beats before racing ahead, pounding against her rib cage. Had she imagined the sound?

"Marly," Pitbull said in a low, ultracalm tone. "Don't turn around. Back up one step at a time, slowly."

"You heard it, too?" she whispered.

"Yes."

With fear tempting her to spin and run, she let Pitbull's voice fill her senses, his calm, reassuring tone wrapping around her like a shield. She took a step backward, then another.

The shadows in front of her shifted, and a pair of eyes appeared and blinked. Another throaty growl made Marly freeze again.

"I'm coming to you," Pitbull said. "Don't stop."

"If I move, he might jump on me," Marly said, her voice low and scared. She could barely breathe for the fear seizing her chest.

A hand slipped around her waist and pulled her backward, behind Pitbull's large, brawny body.

As the animal separated from the shadows, Marly gasped. "It's a leopard."

"Shh. He's coming toward us." Pitbull stood in the cat's path, shielding Marly.

"What are you going to do?" she asked.

"I don't know. This is my first time in a face-off with a wild animal."

"Well, you can't sacrifice yourself. Let's move toward the house." She hooked her hand into the back of his trousers' waistband and tugged him backward toward the house.

The faster they moved the quicker the leopard followed, emitting another low growl.

Pitbull planted his feet in the gravel path. "He might think we're running away. Running will only make him chase us. You get to the house and alert the guys. I'll block the leopard and keep him from coming after you."

"I'm not leaving you to die." Marly tried to step around him. "Let me block him while *you* go for help. You're not wearing heels and can get there and back faster. And, if I need to, I'll shed these heels and run."

While they stood arguing about who should

go, the leopard stalked toward them, closing the distance a step at a time.

When he was within leaping distance, Pitbull balled his fists and sank into a fighting stance.

"Seriously, Pitbull? What are you going to do? Punch it in the face?"

"I didn't bring my rifle. Do you have any other ideas?"

The leopard sank into a crouching position, its eyes narrowing.

Marly wanted to throw herself in front of Pitbull, but he had her pinned behind him with one arm while preparing to throw a punch with the other.

Bracing herself for the attack, Marly was surprised when the leopard rose to all fours and walked toward them, seemingly calm. As he approached Pitbull's legs, he leaned forward and sniffed.

Pitbull and Marly remained still, not moving or talking.

The big cat slinked closer and rubbed his cheek on the side of Pitbull's pants, making a rumbling sound like a muffled motor.

"Is that cat purring?" Marly asked.

"I sure hope so," Pitbull said.

"Mr. Wiggins!" a female voice said from behind Marly. "Oh, dear. There you are."

Marly glanced back over her shoulder to see Talia standing in the open doorway of the house. "Is Mr. Wiggins bothering you two?" she called out. "He has a habit of hiding when new guests arrive. I've been looking all over for him."

"You mean he's not wild?" Marly asked, her voice shaking.

Talia laughed. "Yes and no. Yes, he's a wild animal, but no, we raised him from a cub. His mother was killed by poachers. He would have died had we not taken him in."

Mr. Wiggins rubbed against Pitbull's leg, then Marly's, and finally headed toward Talia.

She leaned down and scratched the big guy beneath the chin. "I'm sorry. I should have warned you. He's fairly harmless."

Marly laughed, the sound wobblier than she would have liked. "Fairly?"

"Oh, you know, he's big enough to knock someone down when he's playing."

No, Marly didn't know, but she'd take Talia's word for it.

Pitbull took her hand, pulled her against his side and faced Talia. "Thank you for clarifying."

Talia straightened, her eyebrows rising. "You didn't think... Oh, I really am sorry. How disconcerting to see a wild leopard coming out of the rosebushes when I'd said the garden was perfectly safe." She waved them toward the house. "Come in and let me get you a drink."

Pitbull shook his head. "No, thank you. We came out to enjoy the stars and roses." He tightened his hold on Marly. "Unless you want to go in."

She shook her head. "No, I'd like to see those roses we came out to enjoy."

"Then don't let me and Mr. Wiggins keep you." Talia bent to the big cat. "You're so very naughty. Get in here." She held the door for Mr. Wiggins. Once his six-foot-long body passed through, she had to wait for the three feet of tail to clear before she could close the door.

Finally alone again, Marly glanced up at Pitbull and burst out laughing.

He chuckled slowly at first, then laughed louder along with her.

The sexually charged, tense mood of earlier had passed, along with the fear of being ripped apart by a wild beast.

Pitbull held out a hand. "Let's see those roses."

She placed her palm in his and they walked through the garden in companionable silence.

Marly found herself chuckling again.

"What's so funny?" Pitbull asked.

She shook her head. "I really thought Mr. Wiggins was going to have us for a snack."

"You and me both." Pitbull stopped in the archway of a rose-laden arbor. He pulled her into his arms, his hands resting at the small of her back. "I didn't want it to end that way between us."

"You and me both," she repeated and looked up into his eyes. "You were right, though." She cupped his cheek.

"I was?"

"Yes." She brushed a thumb across his lips. "Anything between us would never last."

"It really is too bad." He captured her hand in his and brought it to his lips. "I like the way you laugh."

Her breath caught as he pressed his lips to her fingertips. "And I like the way you kiss." She sighed. No use dragging it out any longer than they already had. "Well, I guess it's time to call it a night." She leaned up on her toes and pressed a kiss to his cheek. "Thank you for the walk in the garden."

Before he could stop her, she pulled free of his grip and hurried back to the house. In the back of her mind, Marly pictured her exit another way. She imagined Pitbull running after her, telling her that he couldn't let their passion end so abruptly and he wanted her to be a permanent part of his life.

But he didn't. She entered the house, wishing for something she knew would never happen. Her best course of action would be to steer clear of the SEAL, get her plane fixed and get on with her life.

Her cold, lonely life.

Alone.

Wow. She'd never thought of it that way before she met Pitbull. Now she couldn't think of it any other way.

Pitbull remained in the garden for a short time after Marly left. He'd been tempted to rush after her and beg her not to go to her room, but to come with him to his bungalow, where they could spend the night making passionate, meaningless love into the wee hours of the morning.

He had no doubt that despite her claim to be inexperienced, she'd be an ardent lover, eager to learn and try new things. Pitbull knew making love to Marly would only make him fall in love with the woman and possibly make her fall for him. And what would that get either of them? Heartache, loneliness and depression.

He had a job to do with the US Navy. He never knew where he'd be deployed next or when. Not only that, he was based out of Virginia, across a wide ocean from Africa. He couldn't ask Marly to give up her life on a different continent to be a navy wife, waiting in Virginia for her man to return. She wasn't the type of person who could sit around a house or apartment waiting. It would drive her crazy in the first week, much less the months he could be gone.

Add to the absences the likelihood of returning home in a body bag. A navy SEAL's job was all about danger. They went into enemy-infested places on some of the most dangerous missions. Coming back alive was never a guarantee.

And, hell, the woman was a pilot. She could die just as easily in a plane crash.

An image of his father placing flowers on his mother's grave passed through Pitbull's memories. No, he couldn't put himself through that kind of heartache, either.

He tipped his head toward the moon shining down on him. Why was he even thinking long-term about Marly? He'd known her two weeks, tops, and only on the few flights she'd taken him on. Today, he'd gotten to know her on a more personal basis, and he liked her even more afterward. Especially the way her body fit against his. She wasn't short like most of the women he'd dated. She was tall and slender and kissed like nobody's business. If her reaction to his kiss was an example of her inexperience, he'd take an inexperienced woman any day! His lips still burned with the need to kiss her again.

What he wanted was more time with Marly. But that would be foolish. After this week, they'd go their separate ways. She'd fly her plane in the African bush, and he'd return to Djibouti or some other mission the navy saw fit to assign him to.

Thank goodness he and his team were

going on safari tomorrow. He'd have all day with the heat and dust to drive Marly out of his mind. By the time they returned, he'd have his head on straight again. And then, with the distance, he'd get over her soon enough.

With that plan in mind, he returned to the house, stepping through the back door. He could hear his teammates laughing and talking loudly in the game room. He thought about joining them, but changed his mind and headed for the front entrance. He'd gone only three steps when Buck emerged from the game room, smiling and throwing a comment over his shoulder. "Told you we were unstoppable." He caught sight of Pitbull and hurried over to sling an arm over his shoulder. Buck's breath smelled of liquor.

"Booze good?" Pitbull asked.

"Had to drink to give the other team a handicap." Buck chuckled. "We still won."

"Headed to your bungalow?" Pitbull asked.

"That I am, buddy. That I am." He walked toward the front entrance, leaning heavily on Pitbull. "Marly came in from the garden by herself. You two break it off?"

Pitbull stiffened as he reached for the knob

and pulled the heavy wooden door open. "Who said we had anything to break off?"

Buck stepped through the door and slammed a hand to Pitbull's chest. "Seriously, man. The game room windows overlook the garden. You two were sucking face like a couple of teenagers. Kinda hard to miss."

Great. Pitbull helped Buck keep his balance as they descended the steps to the ground. He'd be the target of every joke the next day. Forcing a nonchalance he didn't feel, he shrugged. "So?"

"When Marly came in by herself, we figured you blew it."

His lips twisting, Pitbull fought the urge to hit something. Namely his friend. "Thanks for your vote of confidence."

"No worries, buddy. I tried to give you a second chance to fix whatever you broke with her."

"How's that?"

"I invited her to join us on the safari tomorrow." Buck grinned as they came to a stop in front of his bungalow. "This is my stop. Thanks for walking me home. Do you want a kiss good-night for your trouble?" Buck winked.

"Hell, no." Pitbull shoved the man toward his door. "Go to bed and sleep the booze off. We have a long day ahead of us."

And an even longer night. Not only was he assured of dreaming about the woman, he'd have her with him and his team throughout the next day. There would be no escape or distance to allow him to get over Marly.

Thanks, Buck. Remind me to return the favor someday.

"About Marly." Buck hesitated at his door.

Pitbull tensed. "What about Marly?"

Buck's brows knitted. "She turned us down. It seems Ms. Marly would prefer to tinker with her plane than vacation with a bunch of mangy SEALs. Night, dude."

With a mixture of relief and disappointment, Pitbull entered his cabin, stripped and climbed into the comfortable bed. He lay for a long time with his arms crossed behind his head, staring up at the ceiling.

Thankful he wouldn't have to be with Marly the next day, he couldn't understand why he suddenly had the urge to cancel his spot on the safari. Staying back at the resort would defeat the purpose of getting Marly out of his head. He rolled over and punched the pillow.

He could have had Marly in his bed. Instead, he was sleeping alone tonight. That is, if he actually got any sleep.

The warmth of her body lingered in every place it had touched his. And the more he thought about her, the harder he got.

Well, hell. So much for sleep.

Chapter Six

Marly originally hadn't planned to go on the safari with the SEAL team. She wanted to check on her plane and make sure the local poachers hadn't discovered it and looted everything they could pull, yank or drag from the wings, engine and interior. When she'd gone to Talia before heading to bed, she'd asked if she could borrow a vehicle.

The resort owner shook her head. "I just sent one of my guys into the nearest town for supplies. He took a truck. I have the one we'll be using tomorrow for the safari, and our other truck isn't working right now. It's with a mechanic. So that leaves us with one truck until the other one gets back late this afternoon."

Marly tried not to show her disappointment. "I see."

Talia's face brightened. "On the safari, we'll be going through the area where you hid your plane. You can ride along with us, and we'll make sure we stop to check on it."

Marly didn't want to intrude on the SEALs' safari, but she was worried about her plane. If joining their safari was the only way to get to her plane, she'd have to go.

She'd planned on spending her day away from Pitbull, hoping having him out of sight would get him out of her mind. Apparently, that wasn't to be an option. She resigned herself to being in Pitbull's company all day, and headed for bed.

Though the air-conditioner kept the house cool, Marly tossed and turned, throwing off the covers and then freezing. Hot, sultry dreams plagued her throughout the night, reminding her of what she'd brazenly offered the man—and what he'd so callously declined.

Marly hoped Pitbull was as sleepless as she was. It would serve him right for rejecting her offer.

Before dawn, she gave up on any pretense of sleep, crawled out of the comfort of the bed and dressed in her favorite pink bra, flight suit and boots. Thankfully, someone had laundered her only outfit, then returned it by before she'd gone to bed the previous evening. After performing her morning ablutions, she went in search of coffee.

Marly followed the scent of fresh bread and bacon to the kitchen on the first floor. She smiled as she passed Mr. Wiggins lounging like a regular house cat on the cool tile of the front foyer.

The kitchen was huge and equipped with everything a chef would want to add to a wish list. A man with a white chef's hat stood in the center manning two skillets, deftly scrambling eggs and frying bacon at the same time.

"Looking for coffee?" Talia entered the kitchen behind Marly. She wore her uniform-like khaki slacks tucked into leather riding boots and a khaki shirt with All Things Wild embroidered above the right breast pocket. She appeared well rested, her hair combed and her makeup minimal but evident.

Did she ever show up disheveled?

Marly swallowed her catty thoughts about the woman who'd welcomed her without question and offered to lend her clothing and toiletries for her stay. What little Marly owned was stashed in her one-bedroom apartment in Nairobi, Kenya. "I'd give my right arm for a cup."

Talia led her to the coffeemakers, poured a cup and handed it over. "I have some clothes you could borrow for the safari, if you like."

With her hands wrapped around the warm mug, Marly inhaled the fragrant brew and smiled. "Thanks, but I like my flight suit."

"Could get hot out there." Talia poured another cup and set the pot back on the burner.

"I'll manage. Thanks to one of your staff, the suit is clean."

Talia nodded. "It was the least I could do. The fact you landed that plane where you did was amazing."

Marly shrugged. "I've landed in worse spots. There's not always a landing strip where I go."

The other woman shook her head. "I don't know how you do it. I'm a nervous wreck when I fly."

"It's second nature to me. My father started me flying when I was barely tall enough to see out the windshield of his old plane. He flew people all over Africa when there weren't that many planes flying. I rode in the copilot's seat for many of his flights."

"Got more coffee where that came from?" Big Jake entered the kitchen, filling the space with his broad shoulders.

Soon the rest of the SEAL team were standing in the kitchen, waiting for Talia to pour enough coffee to give each one a mug.

Marly stood back, observing all of the men, but one in particular.

Pitbull. He had yet to make eye contact with her. But that was okay. She wasn't sure how she'd react when he did. She could quite possibly melt into the tile of the kitchen floor. Or she could keep herself together and pretend he meant nothing to her.

Talia waved her arm toward the door. "My chef has prepared a hearty breakfast for you. I'm sure he'd like to have his kitchen to himself to complete preparations. If you'd care to adjourn to the dining room, we can get this day underway."

The men shuffled into the dining room, joking and jostling as they went.

Marly was mildly disappointed and a little angry when it was Big Jake, not Pitbull, who held her chair for her. Pitbull had chosen a seat at the end of the table, opposite from her.

If that was the way he wanted it, so be it.

Marly could easily have handled her own chair, but she smiled up at Big Jake and thanked him for helping her. He settled in the seat beside her and talked to her throughout the meal.

After the fluffy scrambled eggs and bacon were consumed, along with a hefty number of Danishes, Talia pushed back her chair and stood.

The men followed her lead and stood as one, coming to attention.

"The truck leaves in fifteen minutes," Talia said. "The earlier we get out there, the more we'll see."

"We'll be ready," Big Jake assured her.

She sent an inclusive smile toward Marly. "Oh, and Ms. Simpson will be joining us."

At Talia's announcement, Pitbull's gaze shot toward Marly. He didn't appear to be too pleased. Marly couldn't agree more. She really needed the distance from the man who turned her insides to mush. Still, his apparent shock disturbed her. She raised her brows and met his stare head-on. If he didn't want her to go, he could speak up.

After a long moment, he turned and walked away.

Marly considered that a win on her part.

Not that she felt like she'd won anything of value, but she refused to back down from any challenge, real or perceived.

So he wasn't happy she was coming on the safari. Tough!

PITBULL HAD SPENT a rough night tossing and turning, his libido so jacked up he couldn't find relief from his urges or the heat of the savanna night. He'd finally fallen asleep in the wee hours of the morning, only for his alarm to go off a couple hours later. He'd looked forward to riding around, looking at the amazing animals Africa had to offer, free of the one person who had his insides knotted since that kiss the night before.

But no.

Marly was going with them.

Part of him was happy. The other part tightened like a rope in a tug-of-war contest between bulldozers. He'd be sure to ride in the back of the truck, away from Marly and temptation.

He'd hurried back to his bungalow for a hat and his weapon. When he returned, a guard had taken the driver's seat inside the crew cab of the two-ton truck and Talia sat in the passenger seat, holding a microphone in her hand. A canvas awning had been stretched over the wooden ribs, giving the people in the rear much-needed shade for when the sun beat relentlessly down on them later in the day.

Two guards, packing submachine guns, were seated in the back, near the tailgate. Marly sat forward near the cab.

"Wouldn't you be better off riding in the cab?" he asked her as he climbed up the tailgate, into the rear of the truck.

"I'm fine here," she responded.

T-Mac, Buck, Big Jake, Diesel and Harm climbed up behind Pitbull, forcing him closer, until his only choices were to sit across from Marly or beside her. Rather than touch her, he sat across, careful not to let their knees bump. As soon as the truck lumbered into gear, he knew he'd be fighting a losing battle.

Every pothole sent him sliding in his seat, his knees knocking into Marly's, sending all kinds of electrical currents racing across Pitbull's nerves. Good Lord, how was he going to survive the day without going stark-raving mad?

The first few times they connected, Marly's

gaze shot up to his. Then just as quickly, she dropped her eyelids and hid her expression.

But he'd seen it. The recognition and response to their connection. Though she'd given him the cold shoulder this morning at breakfast, she couldn't hide the flare of fire in her eyes when they'd bumped knees. And based on her desire to further their relationship the night before, she had to be feeling something.

Talia's voice came over the intercom. "If you look to our left, you'll see a pride of lions lounging in the shade of that tree. We'll slow down to give you time to view."

The truck lumbered to a near standstill. Everyone in the back pivoted to stare at the trees. Pitbull's knees bumped Marly's once more, but she didn't seem to notice. Her attention remained focused on the shadows where a pride of tawny lions lay.

His teammates had their cell phones out and were snapping pictures. T-Mac had a high-resolution digital camera with a zoom lens, taking close-ups. Pitbull had decided, even before they left Djibouti, that he'd get copies of T-Mac's pictures. He'd take better quality images than anything Pitbull could. Since he wasn't trying to capture images of the lions, he was able to really see them and enjoy studying the antics of a couple of small cubs.

"You must be used to these glimpses of nature," Buck said to Marly.

"I'm familiar with them." She smiled. "I never get tired of seeing the variety of animals, and I never lose sight of the fact that they are wild."

"Oh, look ahead of us. There's a small herd of elephants," Talia said. The truck lurched forward and the people in the back held on to their seats.

Pitbull couldn't see what lay in front of the cab.

The truck rumbled across the terrain, hurrying to catch up with the pachyderms.

All of a sudden, the truck skidded to a stop.

"Everyone, please stay in the truck," Talia said, her voice tense over the speaker.

The two guards in the rear of the vehicle jumped down and ran to either side of the cab doors. Once they leaped up on the running boards, holding on with one hand and gripping their weapon in the other, the truck edged forward and stopped again. The engine grumbled and shut off.

For a moment, the silence was deafening after the loud rumble of the truck's diesel engine. But the silence didn't last long. The crack of gunfire sounded, followed by the desperate trumpeting of elephants.

All six of the SEALs leaned out of the sides of the truck, craning their necks to locate the source of the gunfire.

"We have poachers in the area," Talia said over the speaker. "Please remain seated. We'll get you back to the resort immediately."

"Wait!" T-Mac yelled. "We can't let them kill the elephants."

"Right. We have to do something," Big Jake agreed.

"I can't afford to have my guests die on my watch," Talia said, then directed the driver to turn the truck around.

As the vehicle slowed in the turn, the SEALs jumped out, two at a time.

The truck stopped and Talia dropped to the ground. "What are you doing? Get back in the truck."

"We can't let them kill those animals," Diesel said.

"You'll get yourselves killed trying to stop them." Talia shook her head. "Not only would that be bad for my business, but I kind of like you guys in one piece."

Big Jake pulled his handgun from beneath his loose shirt and checked the magazine. "We know how to take care of ourselves."

Talia stared from one man to the next. "Poachers play for keeps. If they get a chance, they'll kill you. And if they don't kill you, the elephants are stirred up. They might decide you're as much a threat as the poachers, and stampede. Please. Get back in the truck."

"No can do, ma'am," T-Mac said.

Big Jake held the passenger door for Talia. "Ma'am, you need to take the truck and Ms. Marly, and get far enough away that you don't get caught in the crossfire." He nodded toward Pitbull. "Stay with them in case something happens and trouble heads your way. They need your protection. Get them to safety."

When Talia made no move to get back into the truck, Big Jake's hands circled her waist and he lifted her into the seat.

Talia glared. "I'm not going to talk you out of this, am I?"

"No, ma'am," Big Jake said. He tipped his chin toward Pitbull.

Pitbull wanted to be in on the action, and

they needed to put a stop to the poaching, but he was just as concerned for the women.

"I want to go with you," Marly insisted. "I have a gun."

Her words settled it for Pitbull. "Yeah, but you're not going." As Big Jake had done with Talia, Pitbull lifted Marly into the back of the truck.

"At least take the guards with their machine guns," Talia offered.

Big Jake nodded. "If you promise to get the hell away from here."

Talia gave the two guards their orders and climbed into the truck. "Be careful. I don't want to have to explain to the US government why five of their finest were killed on a safari."

Pitbull glanced at Talia. "Do you need me to drive?"

"No, my driver is more familiar with the vehicle and terrain."

"Okay then. I've got your back." He climbed into the bed of the truck, his weapon drawn.

Marly tried to duck past him. "I want to help."

Blocking her exit, he refused to let her climb out.

She crossed her arms over her chest. "You're not the boss of me," she argued, trying to get around him. "I want to help the animals just as much as they do."

"You'd only slow them down. I'm betting you're much faster flying than running." His tone softened. "Look. I care about what happens to the elephants as much as you do, but think about it. You'd be a liability and take the team's focus off the goal."

The five SEALs and the two guards had already taken off through the grasslands, running toward the sounds of gunfire and elephants' screams.

Marly stared after them, her brow furrowed, her bottom lip caught between her teeth. "What about your team? They might get hurt."

"They can take care of themselves." At least, he hoped they could in the face of poachers and raging elephants. Pitbull wished he could be with them to make certain they all came out of it alive. Those men were his brothers.

Marly sat back on the bench and held on as the truck sped away from the scene. Her gaze shifted from the men running toward the problem and back to Pitbull. "You want to be out there, too."

He met her gaze. "You know it."

"But you're stuck babysitting me and Talia." She shook her head. "We're big girls. We can get back to the resort on our own."

"You don't know that. There's safety in numbers."

"Still, you would never forgive yourself if something happened to your teammates." Marly looked back toward the men as they disappeared over the horizon.

"We each have our job to do. Whatever happens out there happens." He nodded toward his team before turning back to her. "And what happens here, I'll take care of you."

The driver slammed on the brakes and the truck skidded to a stop, throwing Marly and Pitbull to their knees and sliding across the metal truck bed.

An elephant's trumpet sounded so close, it made Pitbull scramble to his feet.

Something hit the truck hard, rocking it on its wheels.

"Hold on!" Pitbull cried.

He dragged himself to his feet and peered through the slatted side panels at the same moment a huge gray behemoth rammed the side of the truck, knocking him backward. He hit the metal floor and slid toward Marly.

They were being attacked by a huge bull elephant.

The truck lurched sideways, tipped up on the left wheels and slammed back on all six.

"We need to get out of here!" Pitbull yelled. Before the last word was out of his mouth, the elephant rammed the truck again, pushing so hard, the wheels left the ground, again. The entire vehicle teetered for a moment and then fell over on its side.

As if in slow motion, Pitbull tumbled, bounced off Marly and hit the wooden bench. Pain shot through his back and hip, and he cracked his head on something hard. Finally, he stopped, flat on his back, lying on the side rails of the truck bed with Marly sprawled across his chest, her face close to his. "Are you all right?" he asked.

She nodded, pressing her hands to his chest in an attempt to sit up.

The truck rocked again, but it wouldn't tip any more. This time when the elephant rammed it, the vehicle slid sideways across the ground.

Marly clung to Pitbull, and he held her tightly to him as the attack progressed.

After several more attempts to crush the truck, the elephant trumpeted and moved on toward the other elephants in the distance.

When the beast was gone, Pitbull looked up at Marly. Her lips were close enough, all he had to do was lean up and…

He claimed her mouth, thrusting his tongue between her teeth in a raw and savage kiss.

Marly's tongue met his in fierce response. For a brief moment they lay still, exploring each other's mouths until they were forced apart by the need to breathe.

Marly laughed. "I thought we were goners."

"You? I was staring the big guy in the eye when he hit the side of the truck."

Marly planted her hands on his chest. "We need to check on Talia and her driver."

As much as he'd rather kiss her again, Pitbull had to get out of the truck bed and make sure the others were okay.

Marly crawled out backward, inching beneath the collapsed side panels and awning. When she was clear of the debris, she held back the canvas and some broken slats for Pitbull's exit.

As soon as he could, Pitbull rose to his feet, shook off the pain and stiffness and ran for the cab. "Talia?"

"We're in the cab," she said. "I'm okay, but the driver is hurt."

Pitbull climbed up on the passenger side of the vehicle, braced his feet on the side panel and opened the door.

Talia stared up at him, her hair disheveled, a red-and-purple bruise appearing on her right cheekbone.

"Give me your hand," Pitbull commanded.

Talia reached up, clasped his hand and let him pull her out of the cab of the truck and lower her to the ground.

Marly was there to steady her as her feet touched down.

Talia turned to face the overturned truck. "What about Henry, the driver?" She stepped away from Marly's hold and rested her hand on the downed vehicle. "Can you get him out on your own?"

Pitbull glanced down at the man still lodged behind the steering wheel. "Henry?"

The driver blinked and moaned. He seemed to be coming out of unconsciousness. He looked up at Pitbull. "What happened?"

"An elephant tipped the truck," Pitbull answered. "Do you think you can come out with a little help?"

Henry glanced at his surroundings and tried to get up. "I can't move."

"Try unbuckling your seat belt," Pitbull urged.

The driver hit the buckle and released the belt, causing him to slip farther down. He grabbed the edge of his seat, dragging himself up and over the gearshift. Once he had his feet beneath himself, he reached out for Pitbull's hand. Between Pitbull pulling and Henry climbing onto the sides of the seat, they got him out of the truck and down to the ground.

Talia hugged the man, tears trickling from her eyes. "For a while there, I thought you were dead."

"I'm all right, ma'am. Just sore." He touched his fingers to the dark skin of his forehead and winced. A lump had started to form and was quickly growing to the size of a guinea egg. "The question is how we're going to get this truck back up on its wheels." He dropped his hands to his sides and studied the problem.

Marly stood near the end of the truck, her

gaze following the direction the bull elephant had gone. "I hope that elephant doesn't decide to trample the men."

The trumpeting ceased and the savanna quieted.

"Hopefully, that's a good sign. Now all we have to do is wait for the guys to make it back to us."

Pitbull wanted to go and see what had happened to the elephants and his teammates. But to do so would leave Talia, Marly and Henry without any protection. Another elephant attack, and they'd all be dead.

Chapter Seven

Marly knew exactly how Pitbull felt. Every glance he shot in the direction his teammates had gone only made her regret tying him down even more. "I'd feel better if you went after your team."

"Yeah, me, too," Talia agreed.

Pitbull shook his head. "No, we have to figure out how to get back to the resort."

"We can walk. It's about eight miles," Talia said. "The radio inside the truck wasn't working. It could be as simple as a loose connection." She gave Pitbull a weak smile. "If I can get back inside the truck, I'll see what I can do."

"Let me," Marly said. "I'm pretty good with stuff like that. I'm always tinkering with my plane, the radio and electronics."

Again Pitbull glanced in the direction his

friends had gone. "T-Mac's the technical guy. He'd have it working using bubblegum and a twist-tie."

Marly studied the overturned truck, searching for a way to climb up into it.

"You really think you can get it working?" Talia asked.

Marly shrugged. "I won't know until I get a look at it."

Talia cupped her hands. "Let me give you a boost."

"Please." Pitbull gripped Talia's arms and set her aside. "Let me." He cupped his hands and bent over.

Marly rested a hand on his shoulder, stepped into his palms and let him raise her up to where she could sit on the side of the truck. "Do you have any tools stashed somewhere inside?"

"Usually behind the passenger seat, but they could be anywhere in the truck now. I'm sure they got thrown around, as well."

"I'll find it." Marly pushed the passenger seat forward and peered down into the cab. "I think I see it."

She slipped over the edge, braced her feet

on the back of the seat and then inched her way into the cab, wedging herself behind the passenger seat and the driver's seat until she could feel the tool bag with the tip of her foot. But she couldn't reach it with her hands. She didn't have room to turn or bend to pull it up.

Once she was sandwiched between the back wall and the seats, she couldn't get herself back out. Marly grabbed on to whatever she could, but she didn't have the arm strength to pull herself up and out. "Great." Looked like she'd have to do just what she didn't want to—ask for help from the man who made her crazy.

Again, she grabbed onto the passenger seat and strained her arms, moving her body mere inches. But if she continued moving inches, she would eventually get out.

A shadow blocked the light from the sun. Marly looked up.

"Need a hand?" Pitbull's voice was both welcome and annoying at the same time.

They couldn't stay out there all day waiting for her to figure out how to get out of a tight situation. She needed to fix the radio and make that call for help. What if the men going after the poachers needed medical attention?

Marly swallowed her pride and nodded. "Yes."

Pitbull reached a hand into the cab. Marly placed her fingers in his.

The warmth and strength reassured her she was doing the right thing. Awareness ricocheted through her body, making it hard for her to breathe normally. The man was sexy, he smelled good and he was oh, so strong.

He pulled her up to sit on the side of the cab.

"I found the bag, but I couldn't bend to reach it." She glanced back down in the vehicle. "I'll have to go in headfirst."

"Let me."

She shook her head. "No, your shoulders are too broad."

"Then let me hold on to you on your way down and back."

"That should work. I just don't want to get stuck standing on my head."

He chuckled and motioned for her to go back into the truck.

Marly more or less dove in. Slowly, of course, but headfirst, walking her way down the backs of the seats on her hands.

Pitbull gripped her hips as she went, and then moved his hands to her thighs and finally to her knees before she reached the opposite door of the cab.

Breathing had become a luxury with Pitbull's hands all over her legs and her blood rushing to her head. As she grabbed the handle of the tool bag, all she could think about was what those hands would feel like against her bare skin. "I'm ready," she croaked as more blood rushed to her head, scrambling what few brain cells hadn't been singed by her lusty thoughts.

Backing out the way she'd gone in was a little more difficult, with the weight of the tools and only one hand to work with.

Pitbull didn't seem affected by any of that. Before she knew it, he was doing all the work and had her out of the cab and sitting on the side before she could tell him she could do the rest herself.

Her cheeks heated and she reached out to steady herself, her hand coming into contact with Pitbull's muscular thigh. If she thought she was struggling to breathe before, she was bordering on hyperventilating now. "Uh, thanks." Marly ducked her head, afraid she'd give herself away if she looked into Pitbull's eyes.

She set the tool bag on the side of the truck and shifted the passenger seat back into position. Then she dropped down inside the truck and stood on the opposite door. The radio dangled from its mount, the wires hanging loose. "I'll need a Phillips screwdriver and a pair of needle-nose pliers."

For the next few minutes, Marly worked on the radio, with Pitbull handing her the tools she requested.

Once she had the wires reconnected, she turned on the radio and tested the mic. The reassuring sound of static filled the interior of the cab.

Within minutes, they had notified the nearby park service, who had a truck and winch. They would be at their location within the next hour.

With Pitbull's help, Marly climbed out of the truck and dropped to the ground.

"Here they come!" Talia announced, her eyes narrowing. "One, two, three, four, five, six…seven!" She beamed. "They're all coming back, and from the look of them, in one piece." She sucked in a deep breath and let it out in a long, heartfelt sigh. "Thank God."

Minutes later, Marly, Pitbull, Talia and Henry were surrounded by the others, everyone talking at once. But before they could tell their stories, the park truck showed up and they all put their backs into getting the two-ton truck back on its wheels. Between the winch, the other truck and all of their efforts, they lifted the truck upright. Talia climbed into the cab and the engine started on the second try.

A cheer went up from all standing around. Harm and Big Jake bent a couple of fenders back into place to keep them from rubbing on the tires. Everyone else worked to strip away the canvas awning and the broken slats. Soon they were on their way back to the resort, the sun angling toward the horizon.

Marly sat beside Pitbull in the back of the truck. She couldn't think past the fact that their thighs were touching.

Every bump made her slam against him until he slipped his arm around her shoulders and they swayed together. After he did that, she didn't notice the heat of the day, the dust swirling around their heads, kicked up by the truck tires, or every bump seeming to chip away at her tailbone on the hard, wooden bench.

Though they all wanted to know what had happened, they agreed to go back to the ranch and get Henry cared for before they shared their stories. Shouting over the diesel engine would have made them hoarse by the time they rolled into the resort compound.

As it was, they searched the landscape for rogue elephants or poachers, on their guard for any other threat. By the time they stopped in front of the resort, they were hot, tired and covered in a layer of dust.

Marly almost wished they hadn't stopped. Having Pitbull's arm around her the entire way had been nice. She wondered if he'd want to hold her again, after they'd had a chance to clean up. Her pulse quickened in anticipation.

ANOTHER VEHICLE WAS parked in the parking area in front of the main house. Diesel and Big Jake helped Henry to the house.

As they neared the door, it opened and a young, handsome man stepped out.

Talia smiled. "Dr. Thompson. Thank you for coming. We had a run-in with a bull elephant and I'm afraid Henry took the brunt of it."

"That's why I'm here." He stepped to the side, allowing the men helping Henry to pass through the entrance. "Bring him into the living area."

"I am quite all right," Henry insisted.

"You might be," Talia said, "but let the doctor check that bump on your head and anywhere else you might be hurting." She turned to the others. "Anyone else injured? Dr. Thompson can take a look."

None of the men took her up on the offer.

"We'll just get cleaned up," Harm said.

"The chef will have dinner ready in—" Talia glanced at the clock on the wall "—oh, dear. In fifteen minutes. Just come when you're ready. No hurry."

Big Jake reappeared in the doorway and winked. "We're SEALs, ma'am. We're never late for chow."

Talia smiled. "Well then, I'll see you in fifteen minutes."

Big Jake left for his bungalow, followed by the others.

Pitbull slowed as he passed Marly. "You should let the doctor check you over."

Although it was nice that he was looking out for her, Marly didn't feel the need to see the doctor. "Other than a few scratches and bruises, I'm fine." She raised her eyebrows. "What about you?"

He pressed a hand to his ribs. "Like you, just a few bruises. I've had worse."

They stood for a moment in silence. The closeness they'd shared on the trip back to the resort seemed to be slipping away, and Marly didn't know what to do to hold on to it. "I'll see you in fifteen."

"I'm sure Talia wouldn't expect you to be ready that quickly."

Marly's lips thinned. "I can be ready in five."

Pitbull held up his hands. "Sorry. I didn't mean to imply that you were slow." He bent to press his lips to her cheek. "You're an amazing woman, Marly Simpson." Then he left her standing there and hurried toward his bungalow.

Marly touched a hand to her cheek and watched until Pitbull disappeared around the corner of the house. She couldn't make heads or tails of that man. One minute he was pushing her away, the next he was kissing her.

Hell. She didn't know where this was going or how it would end, but she did know she wanted more.

PITBULL FELT LIKE his entire body had been tossed around in a rock tumbler. Every muscle ached and he knew he'd be covered in bruises, but he didn't care. He wanted only to shower, change into his fancy clothes and get back to Marly. Damn. When had he become obsessed with the woman?

Oh, yeah. Somewhere between crash-landing her airplane and being rolled by an angry bull elephant.

After a quick shower and a once-over of his body, he shrugged and dragged on his clothes. Bruises to his body he could live with. What about his heart, though? He'd never found a woman he'd even considered falling in love with. What if she got cancer and died, like his mother? Or was hit by a train, or crashed in an airplane?

And then there was his job. He'd be deployed, and she'd get lonely and leave him while he was gone. That's what happened to so many of the SEALs he'd known. Nothing like getting a Dear John letter, or worse, divorce papers served while away at war. Why risk his heart, only to have it broken?

Yeah, he'd be smart to keep this light. Just a fling. No commitment and no strings attached. As long as Marly understood that, why shouldn't they spend the rest of the week in each other's beds? Assuming her offer of the night before remained open.

He dressed in his shirt and trousers and pulled on his boots. After briefly finger-combing his hair, he slung his tie around his neck and left the bungalow. Ten minutes had passed when he found himself half walking, half jogging back to the main house.

"Where's the fire?" Buck called out from the doorway of his bungalow. "Hold up. I'll walk with you."

Pitbull stopped and waited for his friend, a little frustrated at how slowly the man was walking. But he told himself Marly couldn't have gotten through her shower as fast. Women had to blow-dry their hair and shave their legs or something. She wouldn't be ready as quickly as him. No way.

"I heard Talia say you guys had some trouble with a bull elephant," Buck said as he joined Pitbull.

"I'd rather tell the story once when we're all at the dinner table. Same with you. I want to know what happened with the poachers."

"Well then, what should we talk about while we're waiting for everyone else?"

"Who said we have to talk?" Pitbull's concentration centered on getting to the house—and Marly.

"What's with you and our Marly girl?" Buck shot him a sideways grin. "And don't play dumb with me. You had your arm around her the whole way back to the resort. Are you two a thing?"

Pitbull wasn't ready to talk about Marly or what he was feeling toward her. Not yet. He didn't even know where it was going. "We're not a thing."

Buck nodded, his lips twisting as he walked beside Pitbull. "I hear Talia is planning on having music after dinner. There might be dancing. I think I'll ask Marly to dance with me." He tipped his head toward Pitbull and raised his eyebrows. "Since you're not a thing, I figure she's fair game."

Pitbull's hands balled into fists. After the day he'd had, he was one breath short of slugging his friend. Instead he forced a shrug.

"You can ask her." Hopefully, she'd spit in his face and turn him down flat.

"You know, she's not a beautiful woman, not in the classical sense. Not like Talia," Buck said. "But she's feisty and tall. Until she wore that dress last night, I didn't realize just how long her legs were."

Pitbull rounded on his friend and jabbed him in the chest. "You hurt Marly and you'll have me to answer to. Do you understand?"

Buck held up his hands as if in surrender and chuckled. "Just poking the bear. I figured you had a thing going with Marly, but I wasn't sure you knew it yet." He nodded. "You know it now, don't you?"

His breathing came in ragged huffs, anger simmering so close to the surface, Pitbull could erupt at any moment. "Don't push me, Buck. Marly's a good woman. She deserves to be treated with respect."

"And you're just the man to do that, right?" Buck grinned.

Pitbull wanted to knock the man's teeth out, and danged if he knew why. This was his *friend*.

"Hey, what's going on out here?" Big Jake's voice carried to them from the front entrance to the house. "Do I need to break you two up and send you to separate corners?"

Buck waved at Big Jake. "No. We're good. Just getting a few things straight. Aren't we?"

Still caught up in his anger, Pitbull fought to calm the fire burning inside. He nodded and turned toward the house, falling in step beside Buck. "We're good."

"Oh, and Big Jake?" Buck said as they climbed the steps to the front door. "Just to set the record straight, our man Pitbull doesn't have a thing for our pilot, Marly, but he doesn't want anyone else to dance with her. Got it?" Buck tapped Big Jake's chest and ducked past him before Pitbull could take a swing.

Big Jake frowned. "Is that so? You and Marly?" He grinned. "Doesn't surprise me in the least. I knew it all along." Big Jake held open the door.

"What do you mean, you knew it all along?" Pitbull passed through.

"Seriously?" Big Jake shook his head. "You two are all googly-eyed with each other. It would take a moron to miss it."

"Googly-eyed?" Pitbull stared at the big guy. "Since when do you say things like *googly-eyed*? What's happening to my teammates?"

"Yeah, and you're trying to change the subject." Big Jake chuckled. "I'll let it go. But you should know the rest of us aren't blind. We saw you two kissing in the garden last night."

Great. His entire team thought he and Marly had something going on. Well, at least that might keep them from making moves on the pretty pilot until they left the resort.

Why he cared…

Reason kicked in. So many of the SEALs he knew who'd dared to have a relationship with a woman ended up dumped after the first deployment. One guy he'd known had quit the team when his wife demanded that he be home more often. Then she'd dumped him for an accountant. He'd been heartbroken on top of giving up a job he'd loved.

As he entered the house, his gaze whipped to the top of the staircase Marly had descended the night before. She wasn't there. Good. That gave him time to get his act together so that he didn't make a complete idiot of himself.

One by one, the men assembled in the open living area. Talia stepped into the room wearing a black-and-white gown in a bold geometric pattern with black spike heels. She had smoothed back her hair and pulled it up into a modern design that exposed the long line of her neck and her high cheekbones. The petite woman was pretty enough to be in a fashion magazine. But she wasn't Marly.

Talia swept her arm to the side. "We can head for the dining room. Marly will be joining us momentarily."

The SEAL team followed Talia into the entryway and toward the dining room.

Pitbull lagged behind, his gaze going to the top of the stairs again. And there she was.

Marly's gaze connected with his and she lifted her chin.

Pitbull swallowed hard.

The gown she wore was a magnificent, vivid red. The neckline dipped low in a V between her breasts, and a slit ran all the way up, almost to the top of her thigh. Her long, slender leg peeked out from between the folds of the red fabric to showcase a silver high-heeled sandal.

"Holy hell, Marly," Pitbull said, his voice choked with desire.

Her cheeks flushed a pretty red that complimented the gown. "I know. It's too much, right?" She turned and started to walk back to her room.

"No, it's not." Pitbull found himself walking up the stairs. "You just look…" He fought for words that could accurately describe what he was seeing. "Stunning."

The red in her face deepened. "You think so?"

"I say what I mean." He walked the rest of the way to the top of the stairs and held out his arm. "May I escort you to the dining room?"

She smiled. "Thank you. I wasn't quite sure I'd make it down the stairs in these shoes." Marly chuckled softly. "I think Talia likes to dress me."

"She knows what suits you."

"I never was one to wear dresses." Marly gathered the skirt in her free hand and started down the wide staircase at Pitbull's side. "But I think I could get used to it. I've never felt more feminine."

They'd reached the bottom and stepped out across the foyer to the dining room.

Pitbull leaned close. "I still like you better in your flight suit," he said, and meant it.

The men stood around the table, waiting for the last members of their party to join them.

Buck was the first to see Marly. This time he didn't whistle. His mouth dropped open and he simply stared. "Wow."

"He said it." Harm shook his head. "Wow."

"Wow." Big Jake cupped the side of his cheek. "What happened to the badass pilot in the jumpsuit who landed a crippled plane in a field full of wild animals?"

Marly turned away. "I'm going to change."

"No, no. Marly, stay." Talia hurried forward and gripped her arm. "You look absolutely fabulous. I never made that dress look like that. For one, I tripped over the skirt. It was too long. And two, it needed a longer, leaner body to do it justice."

"Darling, you do it justice," Buck said.

Pitbull glared at the man.

Buck grinned. "All bets off tonight, dude. I'm dancing with the lady in red."

"Me, too," Harm said.

"Count me in," Big Jake added. "We can't let a dress like that go to waste."

"Watch out, guys," Buck warned. "Pitbull might take offense to everyone stealing his girl."

Marly shot a quick glance at Pitbull. "What are they talking about?"

Pitbull clenched his fists and held his temper, trying to appear calm when he wanted to land a fist in the face of every man in the room. "We should be seated before the chef decides we aren't interested in the meal he's prepared." He held the chair for Marly, while glaring around the room at any man who dared to sit to her left.

The others took the hint and left the seat beside Marly open. Pitbull took his seat next to her and counted the minutes until they could quit the dining room and go back to the garden to stare at the moon and make out.

"Now that we're all in the same room and we don't have a diesel engine roaring in our ears, could you tell us what happened with the poachers?" Marly said, starting the conversation.

Pitbull liked that she didn't wait long, but jumped in, demanding the story.

"Sure." Diesel popped his napkin out straight and settled it in his lap. "By the time we got to where the poachers were, the elephants had pretty much handled the situation. Apparently the poachers were trying to kill a female with long ivory tusks and snag her baby. They had a truck with a trailer."

Big Jake picked up the story. "They had shot the cow several times."

Marly gasped and reached for Pitbull's hand beneath the table.

"But they didn't use an elephant gun. The bullets were too small and hit the wrong areas to kill her."

"But they shot her?" Marly asked.

"Yes," Harm said. "Which only managed to make her mad. She was calling all of her buddies to come help."

"We circled wide, seeing as the herd had converged on the poachers and their vehicles. They were stomping the crap out of them."

"Like what the bull elephant tried to do to us," Pitbull muttered.

"Yeah." Buck grinned. "I'd like to hear that story."

"Next." Pitbull waved his hand. "Continue."

"The poachers were aiming out the windows of their vehicles and firing randomly, hoping to scare off the elephants," T-Mac picked up. "We couldn't let them hurt another animal, so we moved in as close as we could get without letting the elephants see us. We figured they'd think we were with the poachers and attack us, too."

"Like T-Mac said, we moved closer," Big Jake said. "We fired at the poachers. They were so shocked by our presence they spun out and drove off."

Buck grinned. "We followed them a little way on foot to see which way they were going."

Talia set her fork on the table beside her plate. "Which way was that?"

"South. Due south," Diesel said. "As fast as they could go. When we turned around to come back, the herd of elephants were in the way, and they were twitchy."

"By then, the big bull had joined them and stirred the womenfolk up again," Buck said. "They didn't seem to want to settle down."

"Bottom line, we had to swing really wide to stay out of their sight and out of charging distance." Big Jake grinned. "I don't know what you did to that bull, but he was madder than hell."

"Yeah." Buck stared across the table at Pitbull and Marly. "What did you do to make him so mad?"

Marly laughed. "We crossed his path."

"No, really. Did you poke him?" Buck asked. "Or did you tweak his nose hairs? Because that dude came lumbering in, trumpeting as loud as a trombone player on steroids."

"Then we came back and found you had tipped the truck over," Buck said, laughing. "How?"

"Well, for one, *we* didn't tip it over," Pitbull said. "That bull elephant must have heard the distress calls of his female harem, because he came running, determined to shut down anything that might scare or harm his girls."

"To keep his women safe, he displayed his powerful alpha male side and tipped the truck over?" Buck pressed a hand to his chest. "A guy after my own heart."

Pitbull laughed. "Sadly, that's exactly how it happened."

"Holy hell, Pitbull," Diesel said. "An elephant did that?"

"Yes," Pitbull said.

Talia drummed her fingernails on the table. "Did you see the faces of the men who tried to kill the cow?"

"We did better than that," Harm said. "Show them, T-Mac."

T-Mac took his cell phone from his shirt pocket, opened the device and displayed an image of a lot of grass. He enlarged the image and pointed at the middle. "I got a pretty clear shot of two of the guys before they scrambled for their truck." T-Mac pulled his cell phone out of his pocket and zoomed in on the faces of the two men. They wore black clothing.

"They dress like the guys who kidnapped Diesel's girl and hid her in the jungle along the Congo."

"Let me see the picture." Diesel grabbed for the phone and frowned down at the men. "Hell, they could also be the guys I chased off from trying to kill the gorillas we ran into along the Congo. At least, I thought they were trying to kill the gorillas. I wonder if they were trying to steal the babies, killing the mamas in the process." He shook his head. "It all happened so fast and I was just trying to keep them from massacring the entire group."

"Whoever they are, they can't keep savaging the animals," Talia said. "Not only does the All Things Wild Safari & Resort rely on the safaris to keep it open, the animals need to have a safe place to be what they are—wild." She sat back in her chair. "I reported the attack to the game warden. Hopefully they can chase down the culprits and put an end to the killing and stealing." Talia pushed back from the table and stood. "In the meantime, we need something to cheer us up. We've all had a helluva day." She walked to the doorway. "If you'll follow me to the parlor, I've had the staff roll up the carpet so that we can dance."

Big Jake cleared his throat. "In case you haven't noticed, there are only two women and six men."

Talia smiled. "I know. We women will take turns dancing with anyone who wants to dance." She grinned broadly at Marly. "Right?"

Marly started to stand. "I'm not much of a dancer, but I'm game. Besides, I've already been told this dress needs to dance."

Pitbull leaped to his feet and held her chair as she rose.

When Marly stepped around the chair, Buck was there with his arm held out.

Pitbull puffed out his chest and gritted his teeth.

Buck only grinned, hooked Marly's hand in his elbow and marched out of the dining room.

"Jerk," Pitbull muttered.

Big Jake clapped a hand on Pitbull's back. "You're not giving up that easily, are you?"

Pitbull unbuttoned his sleeves, shoved them

up his arms and then stalked after Buck and Marly. The man knew better, but had still stolen Pitbull's girl out from under his nose.

Harm, Big Jake, T-Mac and Diesel followed Pitbull, laughing behind him. He figured they would all torment him by dancing with Marly. Well, he'd show them.

Music wafted through the first story of the big house in a lilting country and western waltz Pitbull recognized.

Buck and Marly were already whirling around the floor, Buck holding Marly far closer than Pitbull could stand.

Clamping his lips tight, Pitbull marched across the bare wooden floor and straight to Talia.

She turned from the stereo system where she'd selected the music and smiled. "May I help you, Percy?"

"Yes, ma'am. You could honor me with a dance." He held out his hand.

"Why, thank you. I'd love to." Talia took his hand and walked to the center of the room.

Not only had Pitbull's mother taught him how to knot a tie, she'd insisted he learn how to dance, teaching him the waltz and the two-step. She figured if he could do those two dances, he would be a keeper for any woman. His mother had loved to dance. Though he tried to give the appearance of being one tough guy, Pitbull had to admit, he'd gotten his love of music and dancing from his mother. He was just careful to never let on about it to the members of his team.

He swept Talia into a spin and danced her over to where Buck and Marly were waltzing to the music. Deftly, he spun Talia out, took Marly's hand and pulled her away from Buck and into his arms, landing Talia in Buck's embrace.

"Hey, she was my partner." Buck frowned. Then he smiled down at his new dance partner. "Well, hello, beautiful."

Talia laughed and danced away with Buck.

Pitbull pulled Marly into his arms. She felt right there. He refused to think past that. He wasn't in the market for a relationship, but he sure as hell didn't want one of his buddies to stake a claim on this woman. He'd sort out his feelings and courses of action later. For now, he just wanted to hold her in his arms.

Chapter Eight

Marly relaxed and leaned into Pitbull, her body seeming to fit against his like it belonged. "That wasn't very chivalrous of you."

He growled. "Buck only danced with you to poke at me."

Marly laughed softly. "Well, thanks. You know how to make a girl feel desirable."

Pitbull's face burned. "Not that you aren't beautiful. Because you are. Hell, you're too beautiful to be dancing with a crusty old SEAL in the middle of nowhere."

"You? Old?" She laughed. "What are you, twenty-nine?"

"Thirty."

"Two whole years older than me." She shook her head. "You'll be getting dentures and a cane before you know it."

He spun her out and back against his chest. "You know what I mean."

"No, actually, I don't, nor do I want to." She leaned her cheek against his chest. "But you smell nice."

"Woman, you're killing me."

"Mmm?" She slipped her hand across his chest. "What a way to die."

He grabbed her wandering hand and held it pressed against his heart. "What am I going to do with you?"

"I told you last night, but you weren't paying attention." She squeezed his hand. "I promise, no commitment, no strings attached. Just you and me, all night long." What did it hurt to put it out there again? She refused to beg, but he wasn't indifferent to her. The ridge of his trousers, pressing into her belly, was proof.

She swayed her hips and pelvis, sliding across his arousal. Yeah, he was fully aware of her, and wanted what she wanted. Then what the hell was the holdup?

Her blood ran cold as a thought crossed her mind. She straightened and blinked up at him. "You're not married, are you?"

Pitbull laughed out loud. "Really? You're asking now?"

"That wasn't an answer." She stepped away from him, her heart sinking into the pit of her belly. "Oh, my God, you're married."

He shook his head. "No, I'm not."

Her eyebrows knit. "Then what's holding you back from taking me up on the offer?"

"Nothing." Pitbull pulled her back into his arms. "Something stupid like the desire to protect you from heartache."

"How noble." She traced a finger around one of the buttons on his shirt. "Nobility can be very boring. I thought you were a risk-taker."

"I am," he said. "When it involves bad guys holding guns, I'll all over that. But please don't make me break a woman's heart."

"How do you know you'll break my heart?" She tipped her head upward and stared at him in challenge.

He kissed the tip of her nose. "Okay, maybe it's *my* heart I'm afraid I'll break."

She smiled, her eyes bright in the light from the chandeliers above. "Now you're pulling my leg. You SEALs are all over the world. How many women do you have waiting back home for you? One? Two? Maybe three?" She snorted. "Break your heart, my big toe."

"I don't have a woman waiting for me anywhere. Up until now, I've kept my distance, never dated anyone more than once or twice before I broke it off and made it perfectly clear I wasn't into commitment. I love my job, but the life of a SEAL isn't conducive to relationships." His hand tightened around her waist.

"You're thinking too hard on this." Again Marly laid her cheek against his chest. "Sometimes you just have to go with your gut."

He slowed, his feet barely moving to the music. The song ended and he continued to sway.

"The music stopped," Marla whispered.

"Did it?"

"Mmm." She pressed closer, not wanting the night to end.

The next song was a lively country and western two-step.

T-Mac stepped up to Marly and Pitbull.

Pitbull shook his head. "Sorry, her dance card is full." He hooked Marly's elbow and led her toward the exit. Instead of walking out to the garden as they'd done the night before, he guided her past Mr. Wiggins in the foyer to the front door and out into the moonlight.

Marly's heartbeat quickened. What did this

mean? Holy hell, was he going to…? Were they going to…? Would he think less of her when he discovered she wasn't wearing underwear?

At the bottom of the stairs, he stopped and took her hands.

She curled her fingers around his, squeezing hard, a little afraid of what came next but more afraid he'd change his mind.

"Relax." He bent to kiss her forehead. "We won't do anything you don't want. Right now, I just want to walk with you in the moonlight, away from the crowd."

"The guys will be down to one female to dance with," she said, her voice shaking and breathy. God, she was a neophyte at seduction.

"Well, Talia seems to be right at home dancing the night away."

Marly nodded and swept her tongue across her suddenly dry lips. "What's next?"

He laughed and slipped an arm around her waist. "We walk."

She let him guide her down the path past the bungalows. Once they were out of range of the lights from the buildings, the moon lit up the sky, the stars spreading out like so many diamonds on a bed of black velvet.

"This is what I love about the wildest parts of Africa," Marly said.

"What's that?"

"You can see the stars. There's not as much light pollution like in the big cities. I could fly for miles and miles and see nothing but stars."

"Do you ever get disoriented?"

She laughed. "No. I have my instrument gauges to keep me straight."

"Unless the engine cuts off the power?"

"I'm trained for all the possible scenarios." She tilted her head and glanced up at him. "Still not convinced it's safer in a plane than a helicopter?"

He shrugged. "I imagine I could get used to it, given enough time in fixed-wing aircraft."

"You'll have to come up with me again."

"I will, on our trip back to Djibouti."

She sighed.

"Why the big sigh?"

"Just thinking about Djibouti." She leaned against him. "Our time together is limited to just a handful of days. Less, if I get my plane up in the air sooner."

"What are you trying to say?"

"When my part is in, I'll be gone."

"You'll be back for the return flight, though."

"Yes, but once you're back in Djibouti, you won't need my services anymore."

"That's sad." He took her hand and brought it to his lips. "You see, in the couple days we've been together, I've learned a lot about you. Most of which I like."

"You do?" She stared up into his eyes, lit by moonlight. "Like what?"

"I like the way the moonlight makes your hair turn silvery blue." He brushed a strand behind her ear. "I like the way you wet your lips when you're nervous." Pitbull bent to press his mouth to hers in a soft butterfly kiss. "And I like you best when you have a smudge of grease on your cheek." He touched a finger to her lips when she opened her mouth to protest. "Don't get me wrong. You took my breath away tonight in that red dress. I'm sure I had to pick up my jaw off the floor at the sight of your leg peeking out from that dangerous slit." He pulled her into his arms and crushed her to him, the evidence of his desire nudging her belly again.

"Dangerous?" She touched his chest, her fingers curling into his shirt, her heart racing at his words.

"Or the scandalously low cut of your neckline." He traced the fabric, brushing his finger all the way down the V. "Babe, you had me so hot and bothered, I could barely swallow that delicious dinner."

"Have you thought maybe…maybe we should just go with it and get each other out of our systems?" She darted a glance up at his face.

"More often than you can imagine." He cupped her face and tilted her chin upward. "I can't get you off my mind."

She leaned up on her toes and pressed her lips to his. "What are we waiting for?"

He laughed out loud and hugged her close. Then he set her to arm's length. "Care to go to my cabin for a drink?"

"I thought you'd never ask."

He took her hand and started toward one of the bungalows, walking at first, then getting faster with each step. By the time they reached Pitbull's bungalow, they were running and laughing.

Pitbull pushed the door open, swept Marly up into his arms and carried her across the threshold.

She tried not to read too much into the gesture. He was caught up in the moment, trying to get her into his bed before she changed her mind.

Like that would happen.

Once inside, Pitbull kicked the door shut behind him. Instead of setting her on her feet, he carried her past the little sitting room into the bedroom.

A huge king-size bed took up the center of one wall with mosquito netting draped from the ceiling to all four corners. It made the bed even more intimate and inviting.

When Pitbull finally stopped at the foot of the massive bed, he lowered her legs and let her slide down his front, his arms tight around her waist.

Marly wrapped her arms around his neck and held on. Now that they were where she wanted him, all of her insecurities rose up to paralyze her. What did she do? Should she strip out of her clothes? Take his clothes off him? She knew she wanted to be naked as soon as possible. But would Pitbull think she was too forward and needy?

She stood back and lifted her chin. "Look. I can fly a plane and land it just about any- where. But I could use a crash course in what

I think we're about to do, before I can fly on my own."

Pitbull's brow wrinkled. "Crash course?" Then his frown cleared. "Sweetheart, go with your gut. There's no instruction booklet that comes with making love."

"No? What about the *Kama Sutra*?"

With a deep chuckle, he pulled her into his arms. "That's just to give you ideas on different positions. You know. To keep it fresh."

"Who takes off their clothes first? Or do we undress each other?"

"I think we need to find that drink first." He led her to the cabinet in the corner of the bedroom. "What would you like? Beer, wine?"

"Do you have whiskey?" she asked.

He looked at her with his eyebrows raised.

She shrugged. "My father taught me to fly and to drink whiskey. I like Scotch whiskey best."

"A woman after my own heart." He poured whiskey into two tumblers and handed her one.

She tossed it back, enjoying the burn in her throat and the immediate numbing effect. Before he'd finished his own glass, she handed him hers. "Hit me again."

"Do you know how sexy you are, standing there in that dress, asking for a second shot of whiskey?" He put his glass and hers down on the minibar and dragged her into his arms. "I don't know what will happen between us after we leave here, but I can't hold back any longer. I have to have you in my arms." He crushed her mouth with his and thrust his tongue through to slide against hers.

He ran his hands over her shoulders and down her back, snagging her zipper as he moved lower. Then his fingers slipped inside her dress and caressed the small of her back, and moved lower to cup her bottom.

Marly's heart raced, her blood burning through her veins. She trailed her hands up Pitbull's chest, loosened his tie, pulled it free and tossed it over her shoulder. Without pausing a second, she went to work on the buttons on his shirt.

Go with your gut, he'd said. Well, her gut said get him naked. And he seemed to be of the same mind, getting her there. Her heart sang in anticipation of making love with this man. He was strong, built like a brick house and so darned sexy, he took her breath away.

Marly tugged his shirttails out of his trousers and pushed the shirt over his shoulders.

He shrugged free and reached for the straps of her dress, sliding them over her shoulders. The dress floated past her hips to pool in a sea of red at her ankles. She stood before him in nothing but the silver high heels she'd borrowed from Talia.

Pitbull took a step back, his gaze sweeping over every inch of her.

Her cheeks burned and she fought to keep from covering her small breasts. Next to Talia's curvy shape, Marly felt inadequate and boyish.

He shook his head. "Sweet Heaven, you're beautiful."

"No, I'm not." She did raise her hands to cover her chest. "I'm too small in some places and too tall to be feminine."

He took her hands in his and brought them to his lips. "You're perfect. More than a mouthful is too much, and I like that you aren't the size of a little girl. You're more my equal, someone who can hold your own in an argument and possibly kick butt in a fight."

"That's not very girly," she said, staring down at his hands holding hers.

"It's extremely sexy, and the kind of femininity I love about you." He raised her hand to his cheek. "And I kind of like the fact you're only wearing high heels."

"Well, don't get used to them," she said with a shaky laugh. "They're coming off." Marly stared at his broad, naked chest and let her gaze travel downward to the waistband of his trousers. "Seems to me you're a little overdressed."

"I can fix that." He let go of her long enough to strip out of his shoes, trousers and socks.

She grinned. "Nice to know I'm not the only one going commando tonight."

"Yet another thing to love about you. I can't believe you weren't wearing anything under that dress."

"Talia told me anything I wore would leave a line beneath the fabric. And good grief, a woman can't show lines beneath her clothing." She gave him a twisted grin. "I really prefer my flight suit."

Pitbull tossed his socks to the corner and straightened. His body was a honed piece of machinery, all muscular with a six-pack across his abs. Not an ounce of fat graced the man's body.

Marly wet her lips and stared, drinking all of him in like a parched creature trapped in the desert. "Yeah, you really know how to intimidate a girl."

"Why should you feel intimidated?" He stalked toward her, his eyes narrowing, his lips slipping upward at the corners.

"Look at you, all hard as stone, with muscles from head to toe." She rested her hands on his chest, reveling in the steely hardness. "Are these real?"

"You bet they're real." To prove it, he scooped her up in his arms and tossed her onto the bed.

"Hey, you don't have to go all Neanderthal on me," Marly protested, though she kind of liked that he could lift her and toss her like she weighed nothing. She doubted many men could do that. At five-foot-eight, she wasn't light.

"You bring out the caveman in me, sweetheart." He grabbed her ankles and dragged her to the edge of the bed.

Marly squealed and sat up.

Pitbull parted her legs with a nudge of his knee and stepped between them. Then he cupped her chin and lifted her face. "Now's your chance to say no. I'll back off and respect your wishes. But if you choose to continue, I can't guarantee I'll be able to stop."

The deep tone of his voice raised goose-flesh on her arms. "Don't keep me waiting. I wouldn't have walked through that door if I didn't want this."

"I don't know what will happen tomorrow, and I don't care. Tonight, it's you and me." He bent and took her lips with his, kissing her slowly as he explored her mouth with his tongue. He tasted of whiskey, and was warm, wet and completely intoxicating.

Marly wrapped her arms around his neck, deepening the kiss. She pressed her breasts to his chest, wanting to feel her skin against his. This was where she'd wanted to be since the kiss in the garden the night before.

Without ending the kiss, he laid her back on the comforter and pressed his body to hers, his staff hard against her belly.

Desire coiled tightly at her core, sending waves of heat throughout her body. She could die in his arms that night, no regrets.

"I want to be inside you so badly," he whispered against her lips.

"I want it, too," she responded, her voice husky, heavy with lust.

"But first, I need to show you how good you can feel." He kissed a path along her jaw and down the length of her neck to the pulse beating wildly at the base of her throat.

"I'm feeling pretty good right now," she said, her body writhing beneath his. "Any better and I might spontaneously combust."

Pitbull chuckled. "Darlin', you haven't felt anything yet."

"No? I could swear I am right now."

He sucked the nipple of her right breast between his teeth and pulled hard.

Marly arched her back, rising with every flick of his magical tongue on her nipple. "Oh my," she moaned. "I see what you mean." She couldn't breathe. Every time she tried, he touched another nerve and made it sing. In the process, Marly gasped and sucked in a deep breath, tension drawing her body tight, like a bowstring.

Just when she thought it couldn't get better, he switched to the neglected breast and treated it to the same enchantment.

By the time Pitbull abandoned both breasts

and moved south along her rib cage, Marly was so aroused she thought she might come apart.

Pitbull never let up. He kissed, nipped and flicked his way over every rib and then lower, to the triangle of hair covering her sex. He kissed the curls, parted her folds and tongued that narrow strip of flesh.

Marly had only ever heard of a man touching a woman there with his tongue. She wasn't a virgin, having had sex with a missionary's son when she was in her early twenties, but she'd never had a man do what Pitbull was doing to her.

She drew up her knees and dug her heels into the mattress, lifting her hips, urging him to continue.

Her blood burned through her veins, her heart beating so fast, she could barely catch her breath. And she didn't care, as long as Pitbull didn't stop.

He slid a finger into her channel, and followed it with another, and yet another, stretching her entrance. At the same time, he sucked her nubbin between his lips and flicked it with his tongue.

"Oh, sweet heaven, what you're doing to me!" she cried.

One more flick and she came apart. Tingling started at her center and spread outward to the very tips of her fingers and toes. Finally, she knew. This was what all the fuss was about.

He continued tonguing, flicking and pumping his fingers until she'd dragged out every ounce of her release. When she came back to earth, she lay still, as emotionally and physically spent as if she'd been running a marathon.

Pitbull climbed up her body and leaned across the mattress to reach into the nightstand.

"Remind me to thank Talia for thinking of everything. She stashes condoms in the drawers." He reached in and held up an accordion of condoms.

"An excellent idea. It's not like you can walk around the block to the local drugstore to stock up." Marly took the strip of condoms, tore off one and opened the package.

He held out his hand. "I can do it."

Marly shook her head. "I want to."

"Let me guess…you've never applied one."

Her cheeks flushed red. "You know too much about me without me even saying anything."

"You aren't hard to read, darlin'." He touched her cheek with the backs of his knuckles.

She leaned her face into his hand. "I'll take that as a compliment."

"You should. Too many women hide who they are. I like that you don't. Marly, you're real." He kissed her and slid between her legs, his erection nudging her entrance.

Marly drew up her knees and lifted her hips, wanting him to consummate their love-making. Wanting him to fill that empty space that was more than physical.

He bent to kiss her again, easing into her as he thrust his tongue into her mouth. He moved slowly at first, then increased the speed, rocking in and out of her.

Marly raised her hips with each of Pitbull's thrusts, matching his rhythm, wanting him deeper and harder.

Soon he was pumping in and out, faster and faster, the sound of skin slapping against skin and their combined moans filling the air.

That same feeling she'd had when he'd been touching her and making her crazy welled inside. Her core tightened, and she dug her heels into the mattress and raised her hips one last time.

Pitbull's body tensed. He buried himself deep inside her, giving her his full length. His body and shaft pulsed with his release.

That she'd brought him to this culminating conclusion catapulted Marly over the edge, and she shuddered with her own reaction. She rode the wave all the way back to earth, where she collapsed against the sheets on a sigh.

Pitbull chuckled and rolled with her to lie on his side, facing her. "Like that?"

"Mmm," she said, not yet up to forming words. What they'd done had gone beyond good. "That could easily become addicting," she whispered, her eyes closed, sleep tugging at her senses.

"Agreed." He kissed her eyelids and the tip of her nose. "Sleep, sweetheart."

After making love like that, surely she could stay awake and figure things out with him. But no, she drifted to sleep, a voice at the back of her mind wondering…

How am I going to let him go?

Chapter Nine

Pitbull lay awake long after Marly fell asleep.

She'd said something softly as she drifted off.

He'd leaned close to hear, but the words were little more than a whisper. She might have said something like *let him go*. But Pitbull couldn't be certain. For all he knew, she'd been having a dream already.

Let him go.

Was Marly already thinking about their separation? The longer he lay there with Marly in his arms, the more Pitbull realized he didn't want to let her walk out of his life. But they didn't have a choice. Their situation was well past ridiculous.

He was a navy SEAL based out of Virginia. She was an African bush pilot. Unless things heated up in Africa, this was likely the last time they'd be together without making great sacrifices—as in complete career changes on one or both persons' parts.

He brushed a loose strand of her hair back behind her ear, the simple touch tugging at his gut. He wanted to do this again. Not just for the night. If he was lucky, the plane part wouldn't be in until the end of their vacation week. That would give him a few more days with Marly.

It wasn't enough, but he'd have to be satisfied with it. He'd make it special. Then when he had to say goodbye, he'd have no regrets.

Right. No regrets. He already regretted the day of their parting. Damn. He'd made the ultimate mistake. He'd fallen for the woman.

He must have drifted off in the early hours of the morning, while the sky was still dark and the crickets still chirped. The next thing he knew, sun was streaming around the edges of the blinds, filling the room with light.

He blinked his eyes and glanced at the green numbers on the digital clock beside him. Eight fifteen. He tried to remember where he was. When he did, he sat up straight in the bed and stared around the room. "Marly?" he called out.

When she didn't respond, he leaped out of the bed and searched the bungalow.

Marly was gone, along with her dress and the silver high heels.

Pitbull jammed his legs into a pair of jeans, pulled on a T-shirt and pushed his feet into socks and shoes. He was out the door without tying the laces. Something inside him told him to hurry or he'd miss her.

He ran along the path to the main house, up the stairs and into the foyer. Voices sounded in the dining room. He ran to the room, hoping to find Marly and allay his fear of losing the woman.

Pitbull paused in the doorway of the dining room, searching for Marly. She wasn't there.

"About time you dragged yourself out of bed." Buck lifted his mug of coffee in a mock toast.

Talia motioned toward the counter against the wall. "Coffee's fresh. Grab a cup and take a seat. The chef made Belgian waffles with strawberries and whipped cream."

"Dessert for breakfast." T-Mac rubbed his belly. "I'll have to do three hundred sit-ups to burn that off."

"For a week," Harm added, also rubbing his belly. "They were delicious."

His team was talking about food when all Pitbull could think about was where Marly was.

Talia smiled. "If you're looking for Marly, she left thirty minutes ago with Henry and the guards. Her part came in, and she wanted to get started installing it before it got too warm. That, and she wanted to make sure her plane was still where she'd parked it. You never know, with the poachers and scavengers who find their way into the protected sanctuaries."

"Is there a truck I can use to go check on them?" Pitbull asked.

Talia shook her head. "I'd like to loan you the truck, but I have only one available, and I have a safari to conduct today with the rest of your crew."

"Are we going anywhere near Marly's plane?" Big Jake asked.

Talia nodded. "We can."

"Then you can drop me off? She might need help," Pitbull suggested. "Besides, that would free up one of your guards for the safari."

Talia smiled. "You and your team have

proven they don't need guards. They can take care of themselves." She glanced at her watch. "We leave in ten minutes. I suggest you grab a bite to eat in that time."

The others stood and pushed their chairs in to the table.

Buck leaned close as he passed Pitbull. "Not like you to sleep late, Percy."

Pitbull scooped fluffy yellow scrambled eggs onto his plate, ignoring his friend.

"Wouldn't be because you were up all night, now, would it?" Buck said.

Pitbull grabbed a biscuit and threw it at Buck.

The jerk grabbed it midair and took a big bite out of it.

"What Pitbull does at night is none of your business," Big Jake said.

"Thanks, Big Jake." Pitbull stuffed a forkful of eggs into his mouth.

"Although, what Ms. Marly was doing coming out of your bungalow at the crack of dawn left me wondering." Big Jake chuckled and ducked the second biscuit sailing through the air.

Harm caught it. "No use wasting good food."

He palmed it and left the dining room with the others, all of them talking and laughing.

At Pitbull's expense.

Marly would be appalled they knew so much about her comings and goings. He'd warn her to be ready for some ribbing when she got back to the resort.

For the moment, he could barely wait to get in the truck and on his way to where she was working on the plane. He hoped like hell the poachers hadn't returned and decided to take whatever they wanted of the plane and its parts. Two guards and one tough woman weren't much against a band of scavengers armed to kill.

He jammed more food down his throat, tossed back a glass of orange juice and ran out the door, headed for his bungalow. Inside, he settled a hat on his head and his weapon in the holster beneath his left arm. He slung his M4A1 assault rifle over his shoulder. He night need it. The rifle would take down an attacker from a lot farther away than his handgun.

The truck was waiting in the drive at the front of the main house, his teammates standing in the back.

Buck and Harm each reached down, grabbed

one of his hands and pulled him up into the back of the truck.

Big Jake pounded on the top of the cab, signaling they were all aboard. The truck lurched forward. The men sat on the wooden benches and settled in for a long day of viewing some of the most beautiful animals in the world.

Pitbull counted the minutes until he could put his gaze on Marly. He didn't like that she was out on the savanna without him. Then he realized, once he was gone from Africa, he wouldn't know where she was at any given time. Her job took her all over. She could be facing poachers, angry villagers and rebel fighters in just about any country on the continent.

"Worried about Marly?" Diesel asked over the roar of the engine.

Hell yes, he was. But he didn't have to let on to his buddies. He forced a shrug.

Diesel's lips twisted into a wry grin. "I swore I'd never get involved with any one woman. Life as a navy SEAL was hard enough without having to worry about someone else. But then I met Reese."

Pitbull glanced over at Diesel. "Who said I was involved with anyone?"

Diesel chuckled. "You've obviously got it bad for our pilot."

"So? Doesn't mean I'm going to do anything about it."

"No?" Diesel's eyebrows rose. "You're going to end it when we leave?"

Pitbull nodded.

"And it's going to be that easy?"

Why wouldn't Diesel shut up? Pitbull didn't want to think that far ahead. He'd handle one day at a time. When Marly's time with them was up, he'd deal with it then. "Look, I don't want to talk about it."

Diesel held up his hands in surrender. "Okay then. We're not talking about Marly and how much you're starting to care for her. I get it. I fought my attraction to Reese when I first met her in the jungle. Over the next few days, I'd grown fond of the woman and admired her strength and intelligence. By the time our mission ended, I knew I couldn't just walk away."

"Why are you telling me this?" Pitbull didn't want to hear what Diesel had to say. He knew a relationship with a SEAL was doomed from the beginning.

"We decided to give us a chance. Granted,

I'll be away a lot, but that doesn't seem to matter to her."

"At least she'll be on the same continent as you, when you're home," Pitbull grumbled.

"Yeah, there is that." Diesel stared out at the grasslands. "If two people are committed, they find a way to compromise."

"That's just it," Pitbull said. "We went into this with no strings attached, agreeing on no commitment."

The corners of Diesel's lips quirked upward. "Yeah. That's how it starts." He clapped his hands together. "I guess you two will figure it out. If she's still working on that plane of hers, maybe we should leave T-Mac to help."

"Marly knows what she's doing, and I can hand her tools as well as anyone else."

"In that case, the guards could hand her the tools and you could go with us on the safari." T-Mac leaned into the conversation. "Let's see what she's got going."

Half an hour later, the truck pulled to a stop in front of the stand of trees, and the men leaped out of the back. Talia and Henry dropped down from the front.

Marly stood on a ladder, her head bent over the engine compartment. She straightened and turned toward the arrivals. Her gaze sought Pitbull's and then shifted to Talia. "I thought you guys would be on safari today."

"We wanted to check on your status before we headed out," Big Jake said. "How's it going?"

"Fine. I almost have the fuel pump in. Just have to connect the hoses and fire it up to see if it works."

"Need any help?" T-Mac asked.

"No, I don't think so," she said. "I'd like to get it running and at least move it to the landing field near the resort."

"How about we stay long enough to see if you get it started?"

"Don't delay your event for me," she said. "I've got this."

"We don't mind. We have a vested interest in that plane starting," Harm said. "It's our ride back to Djibouti."

"Okay, give me another minute while I attach the hoses." Marly's gaze slipped over Pitbull, and then she turned back to her work.

Pitbull wished the others would leave and take the guards with them. He'd like to have Marly all to himself. They had some talking to do after last night. This no-strings-attached business wasn't feeling right to him. He wanted to know what she was thinking. Was she still on track for saying *goodbye, so long, have a good life*, at the end of the week? Because Pitbull wasn't so sure he was on board with that scenario.

With everyone standing around, he couldn't have that conversation. Hell, he'd have to wait. And Marly didn't appear to need anyone's help fixing the engine.

The woman was an amazing mechanic, and damned cute in her flight suit. Pitbull wanted to get her alone so that he could peel the flight suit off her and expose that hot pink bra and her silky, soft skin beneath. His groin tightened at the thought. He turned away before anyone could notice.

A few minutes later, Marly climbed down the ladder, moved it away from the plane and started to pull the camouflage netting away from the propeller and fuselage. Soon everyone was helping to untangle the netting from the plane and folding it up to be stowed behind the truck seat.

"Well, here goes nothing," Marly said and climbed into the plane.

Pitbull held his breath and waited for the reassuring sound of the engine starting up.

Inside the cockpit, Marly flipped through what appeared to be a checklist. Finally, she set it aside and stared out at the propeller. The engine turned over and caught, and the propeller spun.

A cheer went up from everyone standing on the ground.

Pitbull grinned when he saw the smile on Marly's face. She gave a thumbs-up signal through the windshield.

"We might want to step back while she pulls the plane out of the trees," Big Jake said.

Henry moved the truck, and everyone else shuffled to the side.

Marly taxied the plane out of the shadows and stopped. She applied the brake, left the engine running and lowered the cabin door. "I'm going to fly it over to the resort landing strip."

"I'll go with you," Pitbull called out.

"Why?" Buck said with a wink. "She's got it going. Besides, what do you know about planes? You don't even like them."

"A guy can change his mind," Pitbull said. "Besides, if she has any more problems, she'll need someone to provide protection." Pitbull didn't wait for his team's response. He loped to the steps, climbed aboard and closed the hatch behind him. That way no one else could offer to assist. He'd have Marly all to himself.

Marly chuckled as she secured the locks in place. "I thought you didn't like flying." She turned to him and smiled.

"I don't. But I wanted to see you." He pulled her into his arms and kissed her soundly, his tongue pushing past her teeth to claim hers.

Marly leaned into him and deepened the kiss.

Though it was short, the kiss was hot and made Pitbull want so much more.

"The guys can see us through the window," Marly whispered, nodding to the men on the ground pointing at them. Buck gave a fist pump. The others grinned and waved.

"I don't care." Pitbull kissed her again and then set her to arm's length. "Let's get this bird in the air. The sooner we're back at the resort, the sooner I get to hold you in my arms. Without an audience."

Marly settled into her seat and began checking gauges and flipping switches.

Pitbull climbed into the copilot's seat and watched what she was doing. The more he knew about flying the plane, the better he'd feel. At least that was what he told himself.

She clamped on the headset and motioned for him to put on his. When he had, she asked, "Ready?"

Hell, no, he wasn't ready. They would be taking off on a rough field of grass, not a paved or even graded landing strip. He nodded.

Marly released the brake and set the plane in motion. Giving a final wave, she set off across the savanna. "In order to take off, I have to go fast enough to get lift. So hold on, it's about to get bumpy."

It was more than bumpy; it was teeth-jarring and insane. Pitbull held on to the armrests, his fingers digging into the leather.

He prayed they didn't run into a termite mound or anything else sticking out of the ground. As fast as they were going, it would be certain death.

The plane took off, skimming over the tops of several trees as it climbed into the air. They went from wildly jarring to incredibly smooth as soon as the wheels left the ground.

"Better?" Marly smiled over at him.

Pitbull relaxed his death grip on the armrests. "Much better."

"See? You're already getting used to flying in a fixed-wing aircraft. Before long, you'll prefer them."

"If you say so."

Marly keyed the mic and communicated with the closest air traffic controller, giving her destination as the All Things Wild Resort. Within a few short minutes, she set the plane down on the dirt strip and brought it to a stop.

"Not only are you a skilled pilot, but you're also a mechanic? You're positively perfect." Pitbull let go of the breath he'd been holding. "Will you marry me?" He winked.

Marly's cheeks reddened and she gave an awkward laugh. "Don't be silly. People in the bush do whatever it takes to keep things moving."

"I'm betting back in the States they'd require a complete overhaul of the engine after crash landing in a remote area."

She frowned. "I didn't crash-land. I brought the plane down in a controlled landing." Marly pulled the headset off and placed it on a hook over her shoulder. "You should have stayed with the guys going on the safari. I'm just going to be hanging around the pool for the rest of the day."

"Mind if I join you?" Pitbull asked.

She smiled. "I'd love it."

Pitbull lowered the hatch and climbed down from the plane. He held out his hand to Marly as she followed. As soon as her feet touched the ground, he pulled her into his arms. "The pool, huh?"

She leaned up on her toes and pressed her lips to his. "Unless you can offer a better alternative."

"You, me, my bungalow."

"I'm in."

"Good, because I've been dying to peel you out of that flight suit."

She laughed. "I'm the same beneath the suit as I was beneath the dress last night. Nothing's changed."

"There's something about that long zipper and the hot-pink bra that fascinates me." He touched his finger to the metal tab and drew it down several inches, his pulse ratcheting up as he did. "Yeah, it's the zipper."

"Come on." She took his hand and led him across the field toward the resort compound.

"We need to get to your bungalow before we flash the help."

"Now you're talking." Together, they ran toward the gate, entered and were halfway to Pitbull's bungalow when one of the cleaning staff waved them down. "Ms. Simpson!"

Marly slowed to a walk. "Yes?"

"There was a phone call while you were gone." She pointed toward the house. "The man left a message. It's on the table in the entryway."

"Thank you." Marly shot a glance toward Pitbull.

"I don't suppose you can ignore the message."

"I can't." Marly sighed. "I'll only be a minute. Probably just a flying gig for after I drop off you and your men. I left word I'd be here for a while."

"I'll go with you. We can eat lunch before we hole up in my bungalow."

She gave him a weak smile. "Thanks."

Inside the front entrance was a table against the right wall. On it was an envelope addressed to Marly Simpson.

Marly tore open the envelope and read the message, her brows drawing into a V.

"What is it?" Pitbull asked.

Marly sighed. "Can I get a rain check on our plans?"

"Why?"

She handed him the note. "I have to fly."

"Can't someone else?"

"There's a shortage of planes."

Pitbull read the note.

Sick child needs evacuation to nearest major medical facility. Please call to confirm.

A phone number was listed.

"When there's a sick child, I can't say no," Marly said. "It's one of the most important tasks I perform as a bush pilot."

Pitbull nodded. She wouldn't be the person he was falling for if she ignored a distress call. He took her hands in his and nodded. "When do we leave?"

Chapter Ten

Marly checked her gauges and ran through her landing checklist in her head.

Landing gear down.

Flaps extended.

Fuel rich.

"Seat belts fastened?" she called out into her mic.

"Fastened." Pitbull's voice filled her ears, making her feel warm and happy all over. Until now, she hadn't realized just how lonely her life had become. Sure, she transported people all the time, but she didn't have the opportunity to get to know them. And until now, she hadn't met a man she was compelled to get to know better. Pitbull drew her to him like no other.

She glanced in his direction.

Pitbull gripped the armrest on the side of

the aircraft with a white-knuckled grasp. The man was one tough SEAL, had deployed to some of the worst places in the most dangerous situations in the world, been transported by helicopter, been shot at, had grenades and rockets lobbed in his direction—and he was terrified of flying in fixed-wing aircraft. Still, he'd insisted on flying with her today, not knowing where he was going or what to expect when he arrived.

Marly's heart swelled. Not only was he a fantastic lover, he was willing to follow her while she performed her job...on his vacation.

Lining up with the dirt landing strip, Marly began her descent into one of the poorest areas in Africa. This landing strip was a lifeline to the missionary family who dedicated their lives to helping others in need.

Reverend Eugene Thomas and his wife, Hilary, lived and worked in the little village, teaching the inhabitants about the Bible, sanitation and healthy habits. Not only were they bringing Christianity to the natives, they were helping teach the children how to read and write and the adults how to build better homes for their families and much more productive ways to farm.

Hilary had put her nursing skills to work providing basic health care to the people. She'd stitched cuts, pulled teeth and delivered babies when called to do so, never wavering in her dedication to making the villagers' lives better. Now her own son was in need of medical care. The sooner he made it to a hospital, the better.

As Marly slowed their speed, the plane seemed to hurtle toward the ground until just before the wheels touched down. It seemed to float the remaining few feet when the tires kissed the dirt.

Beside her, Pitbull released a long, slow breath. He clapped his hands together once and gave her a tight smile. "Well done."

Marly laughed. "Glad you think so." She taxied to the group of people waiting at the end of the runway.

Villagers gathered around a tall, white-haired man.

Marly stopped short of the crowd and shut down the engine.

Once the propeller stopped spinning, she climbed out of the cockpit.

Pitbull was a step ahead of her, lowering

the stairs. He climbed down and held out his hand for Marly.

She smiled down at him and let him help her from the plane. Sure, she didn't need it and would have made it out fine on her own, but it was nice to be treated like someone special for a change.

They walked side by side to the welcoming committee.

Small naked children gathered around their legs, touching their clothing and hands.

The tall white man extended his hand. "Welcome to Bunanga. I'm Reverend Eugene Thomas."

Pitbull gripped the man's hand. "Percy Taylor."

"Reverend. I've heard good things about your work here." Marly shook his hand next. "Marly Simpson."

"Thank you for coming so quickly. Our son's health has been getting steadily worse since last night. He needs to be taken to the hospital in Kinshasa as soon as possible."

"Any idea what's wrong with him?" Marly asked.

The reverend shook his head. "We don't think it's contagious. No one else is sick like he is. We think it might be a parasite. But he's dehydrated and weak. The sooner they get him a fluid IV the better."

"Where is he?" Marly asked.

"Come with me." The reverend spoke to the people standing around in what Marly had come to recognize as Swahili.

The villagers scattered, running ahead of Marly, Pitbull and the reverend.

They were led to a small hut with a grass roof and dirt floor.

Reverend Thomas lowered his voice to a whisper. "My wife has been up all night with my son. She's very worried." He held back the canvas flap that acted as a door and waited for Marly and Pitbull to enter the small structure.

Inside were three army cots, several trunks and a collapsible desk in army green. On one of the cots lay a teenager. He was long and lanky like his father, but with black shaggy hair. Beneath his tan, his face was pale, his lips dull and cracked.

A woman with salt-and-pepper hair and deep shadows beneath her eyes sat on the cot beside the boy. She glanced up, and relief melted across her face. "Thank the Lord." She bent her head and closed her eyes. When she looked up again, she smiled. "I'm glad you're here. Martin hasn't spoken since late last night. I've tried to give him water, but he's not taking anything."

The boy's situation was dire. A person could die quickly without advanced medical care. And advanced medical care meant taking the patient to one of the big cities with established hospitals and life-support facilities. "We need to get him to the plane," Marly said.

The reverend started forward. "I can carry him."

Pitbull laid a hand on the man's arm. "Sir, let me." He stepped in front of the older man, bent to the teen and slid his arms beneath his back and legs. When he lifted, he cast a worried glance at Marly. "He's very light."

"All the more reason to get him to Kinshasa. Fast." Marly hurried to the door and held open the flap.

Pitbull marched toward the plane, not slowing until he stood in front of the stairs. "Where do you want to put him?"

Marly entered the plane first and adjusted several of the seats. "I had the interior modified to be used to transport patients." Soon she had converted one side of the aircraft into what looked like a hospital bed, sheets and all.

Pitbull carried Martin up the steps, careful not to bump him into the door frame. Once inside, he laid the teen on the makeshift bed and pulled the sheet up over his thin body.

Mrs. Thomas climbed in and took one of the seats near Martin's head. The reverend stood on the steps, looking out at the people gathered at the edge of the field. He spoke to them in Swahili.

They nodded and the older man stepped inside the plane and sat behind his wife.

"Get the door," Marly commanded, stepping into the cockpit. "I'll perform preflight."

Pitbull gave her a mock salute and a grin. "Yes, ma'am."

"And Pitbull—" Marly glanced back at him "—thank you for coming with me."

"Glad you let me," he said.

PITBULL CLOSED AND secured the door to the plane and then took his position in the copilot's seat, slipping the headset over his ears. "Where to?"

"Kinshasa," Reverend Thomas said. "The

General Hospital of Kinshasa is expecting us. I radioed a message to them."

Marly started the engine and taxied to the end of the runway. Moments later they were heading into the wind, picking up speed. Then they were in the air, flying over the tops of the village huts.

Pitbull glanced back at the passengers. They didn't seem concerned about flying in a small airplane. The reverend and his wife were more concerned about their son. Hopefully he'd receive the medical attention he needed in time to save his life.

The flight took just under two hours. They landed at N'djili International Airport in Kinshasa, the largest of the international airports in the Democratic Republic of Congo.

They'd come full circle from a couple weeks prior, when they'd worked on an operation to protect the secretary of defense's son and his bodyguard, Reese Brantly. Now they were on a different type of life-saving mission. Pitbull hoped this time the city didn't blow up in their faces. Last time, they'd barely gotten out of the city alive after an attempted coup against the existing government.

With air travel seemingly in full swing,

Pitbull assumed the coup attempts had been completely neutralized. At least for the time being.

He climbed out of his seat while Marly powered down the engine and performed her postflight checklist.

"There should be an ambulance waiting to transport my son," the reverend said, bending to lift the teen.

"Hold on. I'll carry him down the steps, but first, let me make sure the ambulance is waiting." Pitbull opened the hatch and lowered the steps. He dropped down to the tarmac and shielded his eyes from the glaring sun. Several hundred yards away sat an ambulance.

Pitbull waved and the vehicle began crossing the concrete toward the plane.

Marly exited the plane and raised a hand to her brow. "Good. The sooner they get Martin to the hospital, the better."

Mrs. Thomas climbed down the steps and stood staring at the ambulance. "I've never missed the trappings of so-called civilization more than last night. You don't know how good it is to see that ambulance heading our way."

While Marly slipped an arm around the

woman's shoulders, Pitbull entered the plane, gathered the boy in his arms and eased his way down the steps to the ground.

The ambulance came to a halt seconds later. Emergency medical technicians unloaded a gurney and rolled it over to where Pitbull stood.

He lowered Martin to the clean white sheet.

The ambulance crew loaded the gurney into the back of the truck and went to work, quickly checking the boy's vitals and starting an IV.

Mrs. Thomas was helped into the back of the truck to be with her son. The reverend would ride up front.

Marly followed the reverend around to the passenger side of the ambulance. "Do you need us to wait around to fly you back to Bunanga?"

The older man shook his head. "No. I'm not certain how long we'll be in Kinshasa. But I know how to get in touch with you when we need you." He hugged Marly and Pitbull. "You two were sent by the angels. Thank you." Then he climbed into the ambulance and the vehicle took off, lights strobing as they headed for the hospital.

Marly stared after them. "I hope Martin will be okay."

"Me, too." Pitbull slipped an arm around Marly's waist. "Do you want to stay until we know for sure?"

She shook her head. "If I could do something positive, I'd stay and help out. But I think they will have enough to worry about without me making them feel like they need to entertain me or find something for me to do." Marly glanced up. "We can go back to the resort and enjoy the remainder of the day. Just you and me."

Pitbull's pulse quickened and he slowed. "Unfortunately, by the time we get back, the others will be heading back in from the field."

Marly frowned. "Why so pessimistic? Even if they do show up early, we can have dinner and enjoy the sunset and then call it an early night. They don't have to know we'll be spending it together."

"About that…" Pitbull scratched the side of his neck. "They already know."

"Know what?"

"That you and I slept together last night."

Her cheeks flamed, but she squared her shoulders. "Well, I guess it doesn't matter anymore whether they know or not. It's not like I'll see them again after you leave Africa." She forced a tight smile. "Let's make the most of the remaining days."

"I'm with you." Pitbull took her hand and headed for the plane.

Marly had the airport operator top off her fuel tanks. Once that was complete, they boarded the plane, closed the door and took off for Kenya and the All Things Wild Resort.

"How long is the flight?"

"Two hours, give or take."

He sat back, his mind off the aircraft operations and already thinking about what he'd do to her body when they got to his bungalow.

He couldn't get enough of Marly Simpson, and he planned on making the most of what little time they had left together. At the end of their week, he'd say his goodbyes. He didn't look forward to that part of this vacation. Well, he'd just have to cross that bridge when he came to it.

The two hours passed quickly. Marly made a radio call to the resort frequency, letting them know she was on her way in. When they arrived back at the resort, they were met by Talia's guards and Talia.

Marly powered down the plane while Pitbull unbuckled his seat belt and stepped past her to open the door.

Talia was first up the stairs. "I'm glad you two made it back safely. How was the flight?"

"Smooth," Marly answered. "No problems."

"I'm glad. I almost wish you had stayed a night or two in Kinshasa," Talia said, her mouth turning downward at the corners.

Pitbull frowned, sensing the tension behind Talia's words.

Talia led the way down the steps to the ground. "We had more trouble today."

His gut knotting, Pitbull followed. "Anyone hurt?"

"Buck got nicked on the temple. Our local doctor checked him out. Luckily it was only a flesh wound."

Flesh wound. Another inch in the wrong direction would have killed his friend and teammate.

Pitbull's hands balled into fists. Once again, he hadn't been with his teammates when they'd needed him. Lusting after a woman had sucked every last brain cell out of his head. He couldn't do it again. At the end of the week, he had to let go of Marly or his team would suffer. He had to remain focused on missions.

Marly descended the steps and closed the airplane door. "You couldn't have known it would happen again."

"Yeah, but I could have been with them," he said through gritted teeth.

"After chasing off the poachers yesterday, we thought for sure they wouldn't be brazen enough to come back for more." Talia laughed. "That's what we get for being cocky."

"But you had armed guards and SEALs," Marly pointed out. "Surely that scared them off."

"They were waiting for us in a dry creek bed near the road our safari tours travel on a regular basis. If not for your trained SEAL team, we'd be dead. The two guards wouldn't have stood a chance. And if we had been with regular safari guests, they would all be dead." Talia shoved a hand through her windblown hair. "The point is, don't wander off. They're out there. Waiting for God knows what. I'm putting my guards on a twenty-four-hour watch to protect your plane."

"Thank you." Marly was amazed at the lengths Talia would go to to protect her clients.

The resort owner turned toward the compound. "Come on, let's get out of the sun. It's too blazing hot to be out without a hat."

The path from the runway to the house wound through a stand of trees, providing cooling shade from the heat of the late afternoon.

"This isn't right," Marly mused. "What do they want?"

"I don't know." Talia glanced through the trees as though she could see out to the rolling plains of the savanna. "Maybe they're mad we got in the way of their plans."

"Revenge?" Marly shook her head. "You'd think poachers are always on the run."

"Retribution against a threat they weren't expecting?" Pitbull suggested. "You would have turned around and gone back to the resort to report their activities if you'd had your normal clients on the safari."

"But your team isn't anything like our normal clients." Talia shrugged. "They could have been after your team today."

"Then we could have put your operation at risk by attacking theirs," Pitbull concluded.

"Didn't Diesel say he'd run into poachers in the jungle along the Congo?" Marly asked.

"Yes, and he managed to run them off."

Talia's eyebrows met in a V. "You don't suppose they were the same poachers, do you?"

"What are the odds that the same group of poachers would be in the DRC and Kenya?"

"From what my guys said, the poachers were trying to take a baby elephant when my team stopped them. They had a truck with a trailer big enough for a baby, not a full-grown elephant."

"They could have been after baby gorillas in the jungle," Marly said.

"A ring of thieving baby snatchers?" Talia's lips thinned into a straight line. "Bastards! These animals have enough of a hard time surviving their harsh environment without humans preying on them and their young."

"No kidding," Marly said.

Talia stopped before the gate to the resort compound. "The chef will have dinner ready in just a few minutes. You two look like you could use some time to freshen up. We won't do formal wear tonight. We're having a barbecue, so jeans are fine."

"Great. I'd like to check in with my team first." Pitbull took Marly's hand and followed Talia to the gate.

As they entered the walled compound, Marly pulled her hand free. "I left my logbook in the plane. I'm way behind on tracking and would like to catch up this evening. I'll only be a few minutes. Don't wait on me."

Talia frowned. "I need to get back to the kitchen. I promised to help set up the outdoor tables."

Pitbull stopped and turned. "Go on, Talia. I'll backtrack with Marly."

"Pitbull!" Buck rose from a chair on the back patio and started toward them, a white gauze bandage wrapped around his head. "You missed all the fun."

Marly touched Pitbull's arm. "I can get the logbook myself."

He grabbed her arm to keep her from going. "It's not safe for you to be wandering around on your own."

She shook loose of his grip and smiled. "I won't be alone. The guards are out there, and I have my gun." She patted the bulge beneath her arm. "I'll be back in just a second."

Marly took off at a jog back toward the plane. Before Pitbull could take off after her, Buck reached him and slung an arm over his shoulders. Buck faced the direction Pitbull was staring. "Where's Marly going?"

"Back to her plane for her logbook." He glanced at his friend. "Took one for the team, did you?"

Buck shrugged. "Just a flesh wound. I've had worse."

"I hear it was an ambush."

"Yeah. We didn't see it coming. Being on vacation is making us lazy or something."

"We're not so much lazy as not expecting anything like that to happen," Pitbull commented.

"Yeah, but we *are* in Africa. And we've seen how it's not such a stable environment, given our run-in with the poachers yesterday. We should have been on our toes." Buck grinned. "But we were hurrying toward a herd of giraffes. We were all staring at the giraffes, not our surroundings."

Pitbull grinned. "A herd of giraffes?"

Buck's lips formed a wry grin. "Yeah. They were amazing. I wish we could have seen more of them."

"Maybe tomorrow?" Pitbull suggested. "Surely Talia can locate the herd again."

Buck shook his head. "The gang decided

they want to see Victoria Falls. You don't suppose Marly would fly us down there? I mean, how often are we in Africa?" He paused and added, "On vacation."

"Some vacation." Pitbull laughed. "But it's true. We don't usually have free time when we're on the African continent. I'm sure Marly would take us. All we have to do is ask—"

The crack of gunfire sounded nearby, cutting off Pitbull's last word.

"What the hell?" Pitbull spun toward the landing strip, just out of sight of the house, the trees and all their shade blocking his view. He didn't wait for another shot to be fired. He ran back out of the gate and cut through the trees in a more direct path to the landing strip and Marly.

The sound of an engine firing up made his blood run icy cold. When he burst out onto the dirt landing strip, the plane was halfway down the runway, building up speed as it drew away from him.

Lying on the ground where the plane had been parked were the two guards, unmoving, their arms and legs at odd angles.

Dead.

Chapter Eleven

Marly had run all the way back to the plane, anxious to grab the logbook and get back to Pitbull. With time running short, she had only a few days with the man. She wanted to spend every second of it with him.

The guards stood near the plane, their weapons pointing at the ground. They appeared bored and hot. The afternoon sun beat down on them, making them sweat. Marly would ask Talia for bottled water for them. But first, she wanted her logbook.

She lowered the steps and climbed up into the plane. The logbook was in the pouch attached to the wall on the pilot's side of the airplane. She settled into the cockpit and retrieved her logbook, checking over the instruments one more time just to be sure all was well.

Just when she leaned forward to stand, she heard the sharp report of gunfire.

She gasped and fell back into her seat, her heart racing so fast it made her dizzy. Marly forced herself to be calm and think. Two shots. She'd heard two shots. What did that mean?

Two guards stood outside.

She glanced through the windows toward the spot where the guards had been standing. They weren't there. When she craned her neck, she could see lumps of khaki-colored uniforms on the ground.

Holy hell! The guards had been shot. Marly leaped out of her seat and ran down the aisle toward the door. She had to either get out and run for help, or close and lock the aircraft door to protect herself until someone came to her rescue.

She made it into the plane and was just about to pull up the steps into the craft, when seven men rushed the plane, stopping her before she could lock herself in.

The first one ran up the steps.

Marly planted a foot in his chest and kicked hard.

The man fell backward into his cohorts. The one behind him toppled into the one behind him, but the rest of them steadied the lead men and pushed them up and into the plane.

Marly had nowhere to go. She couldn't duck past them and escape. She had a gun under her flight suit, but one gun against seven armed men would be setting herself up to be killed.

The man in the lead grabbed her arm and spun her around.

She fought against him, but he was much stronger. In the struggle, he discovered her weapon. While he held her arms behind her back, another man yanked down her zipper, removed the gun and pointed it at her head.

"Fly this plane," he demanded, his voice heavy with a native accent.

"No," she said.

"If you don't," the man with the gun said, "he will." He nodded to the man holding her. "And it will mean certain death for all of us."

"I'm not flying this plane," she insisted.

"If you refuse to fly, we will wait for your friends to come, and then we'll blow up this plane and all of them with this." The gun-man pulled a grenade from his pocket and held it up.

She said the first thing that came into her head. "You're out of your mind."

"We are very serious. Fly now, or you and your friends will all die."

"As will you," she pointed out.

"Do it now, before they come." He poked her with her handgun. "We are not afraid to die."

The man holding her lifted her off her feet and carried her to the pilot's seat, where he shoved her down and braced his hands on her shoulders.

Marly didn't have a choice. If she refused to fly, they'd kill themselves, her and the team when they attempted to storm the plane. If she flew away before the team reached them, she would be the only one in danger.

Marly started the engine, eased off the brake and taxied onto the dirt landing strip.

"Go!" The man with her gun bumped her temple with the barrel of the weapon.

"Knock me out and we'll crash into the trees. Now back off," she said, sounding a lot more confident and brazen than she felt. Inside, her stomach churned so badly she feared she'd throw up all over the instrument panel. Swallowing hard on the bile rising up her throat, she concentrated on getting the plane into the air and away from Pitbull and his friends. The farther away she got, the less chance of her captors detonating the grenade and killing the navy SEALs.

The plane picked up speed, racing toward the end of the runway. When she was going fast enough, she eased back on the yoke and the plane left the ground, soaring up into the air.

Marly dared to glance down at the ground in time to see Pitbull run out onto the landing strip.

He'd come after her. Marly's heart swelled.

Not that it had done any good. But it made Marly feel a little better that he would have come to her rescue if he'd been given a chance.

The man holding the gun said something in Swahili and laughed. The others laughed with him. Still holding her pistol, he tossed the grenade to a man behind him.

Marly flinched, waiting for the explosion.

The men laughed again.

"Won't that explode if you drop it?" she asked.

The man laughed again and held up his hand.

The grenade flew through the fuselage and

landed in his grasp. He immediately dropped it into Marly's lap.

She yelped and tried to jump up from her seat. The grenade slipped out of her lap, dropped to the floor beside her and bounced like a ball. The damned thing was made of rubber. They'd tricked her into taking off by threatening her with the explosion of a rubber ball.

She glared, making the men laugh harder.

"Fine. I'll just land the plane." She gripped the yoke and sent the plane into a one-hundred-eighty-degree turn.

The barrel of her handgun tapped her temple. "You will fly this plane to these coordinates." He handed her a piece of torn paper.

She didn't even bother to look at it. "Why should I? You can only kill *me* now that we're away from the resort."

"We have more men ready to attack your boyfriend and his American SEAL team. They do not belong in Africa."

"How do I know you're not lying?" Marly asked. "You've lied before. And how do I know you won't do it anyway? If I crash the plane, I take out the seven of you. Sounds like a win-win situation to me." She pushed the yoke forward, sending the aircraft plummeting toward the ground.

While the men in the rear scrambled to hold on, Marly surreptitiously adjusted the transponder code to 7500, sending out a silent plea, indicating she'd been hijacked.

The man with the gun held on to the seat he stood behind and said something sharply in Swahili.

The big guy who'd originally lifted her off her feet and sat her in the pilot's seat staggered to an upright position, grabbed her beneath her armpits and yanked her out of her seat.

The plane wobbled, but continued to dive toward the ground. The gunman dove into her seat and brought the aircraft under control. Again, he spoke in angry Swahili.

Her captor took off his T-shirt, ripped it into strips and tied her wrists.

Marly tried hard to leave a gap, but the man pulled tightly, the fabric seeming to cut into her skin. "You don't know how to fly this plane," she said to the man in the pilot's seat. "You might keep it level in the sky, but it's a hell of a lot harder to land than it is to fly."

He spoke again in Swahili. The man who'd

torn his shirt tied one of the strips around her head and over her mouth.

It tasted of stale sweat and body odor.

Marly gagged, but couldn't remove it. With her hands tied behind her back, she was limited in what she could do. But her feet were still free.

The big guy had shoved her into one of the seats behind the pilot's seat. She couldn't get away from these men, but she sure as hell could make sure they didn't kidnap anyone else or any other baby animals. After hijacking a plane, they wouldn't want to take the time to release her. Hell, they probably would have killed her already, but they had to get rid of the body. By keeping her alive, they were keeping her body fresh.

All these random thoughts raced through Marly's head while she worked to get the nasty T-shirt material out of her mouth. If she was destined to die anyway, she might as well take them out with her and go down in a fiery crash. Besides, once they did get to where they were going, their plans for her couldn't be good.

Scooting lower in the seat, she drew back her legs and threw a kick at the pilot's head.

Contact!

The man's head slammed forward, bounced against the yoke and back against the seat. The plane shimmied and dipped.

No sooner had she kicked the guy than the big man who'd tied her up with his smelly T-shirt backhanded her with a heavy fist. He hit her so hard, her head snapped back and her vision dimmed.

Still sitting in the chair, she tried to stay awake to keep track of what was going on with her plane.

The man hit her again. Pain shot through her right cheek and she fell back in the seat, slumped against the side of the plane and fought back the gray haze engulfing her.

But she couldn't win the battle, and she slipped into empty, pain-free silence.

PITBULL RAN AFTER the plane, praying it would stop before it reached the end of the runway. No matter how fast he ran, he couldn't catch up. Marly's plane lifted up into the sky.

"No! No! No!" Pitbull shook his fist in the air.

Buck caught up with him, breathing hard

and pressing a hand to his injured head. "What the hell were you trying to do?"

"I couldn't let her go." He spun and walked several steps back the way they'd come and then spun again and marched toward Buck. "What can I do? How will I find her? Damn it, Buck. They'll kill her." He gripped his friend's collar.

Buck grabbed his wrists. "Get a hold of yourself, dude. We'll find her."

"How?" Pitbull dropped his hands to his sides. "Africa is a big continent. They could be going anywhere."

Buck shook his head. "I don't know, but I know someone who might." He grinned. "T-Mac. If anyone can find Marly's plane, it would be our man T-Mac. He's an absolute genius when it comes to computers and communications."

"But it's a plane, not a computer."

"Planes have transponders. Transponders talk to computers somewhere. T-Mac just has to find the computer, hack into it and locate our girl."

"They lose airplanes all the time. What will make Marly's plane any different?"

"We can stand here and discuss the merits

of hacking or actually try something." Buck straightened the swath of bandages around his head. "Come on."

Pitbull ran ahead of him to the main house, yelling at the top of his lungs, "T-Mac, Harm, Big Jake, Diesel!"

All four men ran out of the house, followed by Talia and the chef.

"What's going on?" Big Jake demanded.

"Marly and her plane were hijacked. They killed the guards and took her and the plane."

"Holy hell," Harm said.

Pitbull faced T-Mac. "You can track her, can't you? Please tell me you can track the plane."

"I'll need my laptop and a strong internet connection."

"I'll get your computer." Diesel ran for T-Mac's bungalow.

"Follow me into my office. We have satellite internet," Talia said. "It's fast and pretty reliable."

"What else do you need?" Pitbull hated being so helpless.

"I need to know we aren't going to come under attack anytime soon." T-Mac stared at Pitbull.

"He's right," Big Jake added. "We need to make sure there aren't any other Tangos running around the perimeter or inside the compound."

Pitbull gave T-Mac a narrow-eyed glare. "You're not trying to get rid of me, are you?"

"If I said yes, would it work?" T-Mac challenged him with raised eyebrows. "I need time to figure this out. I've tracked a lot of things, but I haven't tracked an airplane. We don't have a GPS device implanted on Marly or the airplane."

"Do you know anyone who has tracked an airplane using whatever the airplane has on board?" Pitbull asked.

"I have some contacts," T-Mac said.

Talia threw open a door to a spacious office. The walls were lined with bookshelves. A massive mahogany desk stood in the middle of the room with two wingback chairs in front of it and a leather office chair behind.

T-Mac paced the length of the room. "I really need my laptop."

"You're welcome to use my computer." Talia keyed her user name and password and stood back. "Go for it, and find Marly."

T-Mac sank into the office chair and placed

his hands on the keyboard. A moment later, Diesel arrived with his laptop. He set the laptop beside the desktop monitor and fired it up.

Before he started his search, he glanced up at Pitbull and the rest of the team. "Standing around staring at me isn't going to help me find Marly any faster. Please, go take care of the guards before the buzzards do the job."

Big Jake gripped Pitbull's elbow. "Come, we have a job to do, and T-Mac has his job. He'll let you know as soon as he learns something."

"I need to be here when he finds Marly. You don't understand."

Jake nodded. "I do understand, but you're not going to help T-Mac by getting in his way."

Pitbull knew Big Jake was right, but he didn't like leaving, especially if the one man who was conducting the search found something significant that could lead to bringing Marly back. He wanted to be there when that happened. The sooner he knew where she was, the sooner he'd go to her.

Trouble was, they didn't have the transportation to go anywhere.

Pitbull grabbed the telephone on the desk. "Does this thing work?"

Talia nodded. "Most of the time. It's a satellite phone. It can be sketchy during bad weather. But most of the time it's reliable."

"Who are you going to call?" Big Jake put his hand over the one Pitbull had on the phone.

"The team back in Djibouti. We'll need backup and support."

Big Jake nodded. "Let me. You're a little too close to the problem."

The need to be proactive made Pitbull reluctant to hand over the phone. In his gut, he knew Big Jake was right. He was too upset to be coherent and calm. He handed the phone to Big Jake and then hovered beside him for support until he'd completed the call.

"What did they say?" Pitbull asked.

"They're going to scramble the team and call for support from the 160th Night Stalkers." Big Jake laid a hand on Pitbull's shoulder. "They're coming." He turned toward T-Mac. "As soon as we know anything, we're to contact them."

"They need to pick us up first," Pitbull insisted. "We have to be there for Marly."

Big Jake shook his head. "If Marly ends up being closer to them, they'll go direct."

"You're right." Pitbull's fists knotted so tightly his fingernails dug into his palms. "God, I feel trapped."

"And we all will feel trapped until we locate Marly and get a ride out of here to her." Harm clapped a hand to Pitbull's back. "Come on. We need to check the perimeter and take care of the guards."

Pitbull gave T-Mac one last glance. "Find her."

T-Mac saluted him without turning away from the desk. "Will do."

The five men checked their weapons and ammo and then left the office.

Talia followed them into the foyer, her brow dipping into a V. "I need help taking care of the guards. I can't leave them out there for the buzzards to feast on."

"We can take care of them," Big Jake assured her. "I'm not sure how it works here, but shouldn't the police investigate?"

The resort owner drew in a deep breath. "I put a call in to the local authorities. They should be here within the next fifteen minutes." Talia wrung her hands. "Those guards were good men. I have no idea what to tell their families."

"We're sorry for your loss," Big Jake said. "But you might have a bigger problem."

Her eyes widened. "What do you mean?"

"How many guards do you have working this resort?" he asked.

"I had five, but I'm down to three. One fills in for the others and two of them work the night shift."

"It might not be enough," Harm said.

Talia nodded. "I hope I can get additional guards. They might not want to come to work on a resort where two have already been attacked and killed."

"I'm heading out to check the perimeter." Pitbull didn't have the patience to stand around inside the house. As it was, the walls seemed to be closing in around him. The sooner he got outside, the better.

He needed to search the grounds and out around the landing strip. What if the plane hadn't been large enough to hold all of the attackers? There might be more thugs waiting for sundown to make a break for it. If they could capture one, they could coerce him into telling them where they'd taken Marly.

Pitbull grabbed the doorknob and yanked open the door. "Are you coming?"

"I'm coming," Harm said.

"Me, too," Diesel said.

Pitbull stared pointedly at Talia. "You'll let us know if you hear anything from T-Mac or Marly?"

Talia nodded. "You bet. Anything. As soon as I hear."

Pitbull shot a last glance toward the office. He couldn't hover behind T-Mac, and he had to do something to burn off frustrated energy. Until they knew where the hijackers had taken Marly, he couldn't do much to rescue her. He could only kick himself for not going with her to the plane. Guilt gnawed at his gut. He couldn't imagine what she might be going through. Some of the rebel factions in Africa were cruel—especially toward females.

He and his team spread out, taking different directions upon leaving the compound, weapons drawn. After the two guards had been killed, they knew the attackers weren't messing around.

All they had to go on was finding the plane.

What if the hijackers separated Marly from her plane? In that case, they'd be shooting in the dark to find her.

Chapter Twelve

Marly surfaced from a very dark and foggy place. Pain throbbed in her cheek and temple. When she opened her eyes, the darkness abated only a little. She blinked to clear her vision, but the darkness remained as a hazy gray twilight.

She lay on a hard surface, not the soft cushy mattress she'd shared with Pitbull at the resort. Where was she? Confusion cleared as memories rushed in. Marly sat up straight, her vision slowly adjusting to her surroundings. The hard surface was a dirt floor. The walls around her weren't those of her plane. Instead they were made of mud and thatch. The only light making its way into her prison was from a gap near the roof, and it wasn't much. Night must be falling. She'd been unconscious for a while.

Marly staggered to her feet, bracing a hand on the rough wall to steady herself while the world spun in protest. When her legs stopped wobbling, she straightened and searched the interior of her cell for the exit. A wooden door at one end of the small space was the only way in or out, and apparently it was locked from the outside.

She fought the urge to yell and shake the door violently. If there was another way out, she didn't want to alert her captors to the fact she was awake. For a long moment, she listened, straining to hear sounds of movement, talking or anything that would tell her what was happening outside. Several times she heard vehicle engines. Once she heard a shout in what sounded like Swahili.

And then she heard a moan. Soon the moan turned to quiet sobs from the other side of one of her cell walls.

Marly's heartbeat quickened as she crossed to the wall and leaned her head close. From the sounds of the sobs, it had to be either a child or a woman.

"Hey, can you hear me?" Marly called out in just above a whisper.

The sobbing continued.

A little louder this time, Marly called out, "Hey, can you hear me?"

For a moment silence reigned. Then a soft voice sounded from the other side of the wall. *"Oui,"* said a woman with a French accent. French was the official language of the Democratic Republic of the Congo.

"My name is Marly. Do you speak English?" Marly asked, praying the other woman did. Otherwise, it would be next to useless for them to combine efforts.

"Oui," she responded. "A little."

Marly sagged with relief. "Where are we?"

The woman started crying again.

"Hey, it's going to be all right. But I need to know where we are and why we were brought here."

Through her sobs, the woman managed to say, "We are to be sold and taken away to other countries."

Marly swore softly. If these were the same people who'd been poaching on national preserves, not only were they after baby animals, they were involved in human trafficking.

"Oh, no, they won't," Marly promised. If it was the last thing she did, she'd get out of this mess and take the other woman with her. "Are there more women?" she asked.

"Oui," the woman answered. "I do not know how many."

"My name's Marly," she said.

"I am Celeste," the woman answered, though the sound was more of a sob.

"Well, Celeste, we're going to get out of here. You hear me?"

"S'il vous plaît."

Marly searched the room again, even more intent on escape than before. She refused to allow herself and other women to be sold like cattle to the highest bidder and then used as sex slaves in God knew where.

The walls were dried mud and straw, but hard-packed and dense. It would take a long time to scratch her way through with nothing but her fingernails. She eyed the gap near the roof that allowed air and a little light from the moon to filter through. From where she stood, the gap didn't appear large enough for a human to fit through. But she wouldn't know unless she climbed up there and found out.

She'd been over the room several times and found nothing but herself and the dirt floor. Without a ladder or a chair to stand on, she could use only her hands and feet to scale the wall. How hard could it be?

She jumped and made a grab for the top of the mud wall. No matter how high she jumped, it remained out of her reach. With no toe or finger holes, she couldn't climb the wall. Using her fingernails, she scratched and dug into the hard-packed mud walls. All she managed was to break her nails down to the quick. If only she had something hard and sharp.

Marly almost laughed out loud. Too often she'd been poked by the underwire in her bra when it found its way out of the fabric and dug into her skin.

Quickly she unzipped her flight suit, peeled it down her torso and removed her favorite pink bra. A few minutes later, she had the underwire out of the bra. She slipped the bra into her back pocket, sans the wire, and zipped herself back into her suit.

Using the sharp end of the metal, she dug at the dirt walls in the corner of the room, creating toe and hand holds she could grip as she climbed the wall. The work was slow and steady, but what else did she have to do? She wasn't content to wait for the thugs who'd put her here to come back, rough her up and knock her out again. She had to escape and get the others out before they sold them to the barbarians who traded in human flesh.

One by one, she dug holes deep enough and shaped for her hands to grip. By the time the moon had risen high into the sky, she reached the top of the wall and could see out of the building. There was only a four-inch gap between the roof and the thatched roof. Not enough for her to shimmy through but…

She pushed at the thatch. It gave a little but was tied snugly to keep the rain out. Pushing again, she could feel it give a little more. Using the underwire, she slashed at the binding holding the thatch together. The dull edge of the wire did little to cut through. Marly was persistent and kept hacking away, praying her efforts would eventually pay off.

"Marly." Celeste's voice sounded through the wall. "Someone comes."

Marly left the wire hooked in the thatch and dropped down the wall to the floor. She moved quickly to the opposite side of the room, where she lay on the floor as if she were still unconscious.

The door to her cell opened and a flashlight shone in onto her face.

Though Marly peeked through her lashes, all she could see was the flashlight's beam glaring at her. She could hear two guards speaking in Swahili. One of them entered the cell and kicked her with his boot.

Marly fought hard not to cry out or flinch. He'd caught her in the rib and it hurt like the devil. She hoped they'd move on and leave her alone if they thought she was still out.

Her luck continued to be lousy.

The men each grabbed an arm, hauled her out of the cell and dragged her through what appeared to be a small village with a mix of thatch-roofed huts and tin and plywood shanties. Between the huts and shanties were stacks of cages. Some had animals trapped inside.

As they passed by, the creatures locked in the cages sounded off. Some screeched like apes. Others cried like kittens.

This was where they were bringing the baby animals. Marly's chest tightened. Those poor babies, snatched from their mothers, cried pitifully, breaking Marly's heart. Somehow she had to help them and the women who were also being held. It wasn't enough to escape. She couldn't leave them behind.

The guards carried her into the only structure that appeared to have had any thought put into its construction, with sturdy wooden walls and a tin roof.

Marly didn't make it easy on the men. She relaxed her body, still pretending to be unconscious. When they dumped her on the ground in front of a table and chair, she lay still, hoping whoever she'd been brought to see would have them take her back to her cell to recover. Surely they wouldn't sell an unconscious woman?

"Ms. Simpson, I know you are awake," a man said.

She refused to acknowledge him, lying as still as possible, her eyes opened only enough for her to see through her lashes. Not that she saw more than a pair of boots and legs beneath the desk.

The man spoke in rapid Swahili to the two guards who'd dumped her on the floor. They bent to lift her again and plunked her into a chair, and then moved it to sit in front of the table. The tied her to the chair and left her to face their boss.

A single light hung suspended from the ceiling over the table and chairs. The man on the other side wore a boonie hat. The light hitting the brim cast his face in a deep, dark shadow.

"Ms. Simpson, cooperate and I might let you live." He had an accent that didn't sound like any in Africa. He wasn't South African or British. Hell, he sounded American.

Marly sat tied to the chair, her head hanging, her body limp. She didn't know how long she could pretend to be unconscious, but she didn't have another plan.

The man again spoke to the guards. One left the building and returned a moment later carrying a bucket.

Before she could guess his intention, he tossed the contents of the bucket at her.

Water hit her full in the face. The shock made her gasp and she sucked some in, resulting in a fit of coughing that destroyed her ruse of being unconscious.

Marly shook the wet strands of hair out of her face and glared across the table at the man with the shadowed face. "What do you want?"

The edge of his mouth turned up in a smile, the corner of which escaped the shadow.

"That's better. Now that I have your attention, tell me all you know about the American SEALs you brought to Kenya."

She spit at the man's face. The bastard wasn't getting anything from her.

A sharp command from the man behind the desk yielded an explosive backhand that caught her chin and knocked her backward, chair and all.

Marly slammed against the floor, her head bouncing off the dirt. She lay still for only a moment, pain radiating from her chin and the back of her head.

Then she was jerked upright again before the table. Her head spun and she fought the bile roiling up her throat.

"You will tell me why you've transported these men from one country to another in Africa. What is their mission? Why are they here?"

Clamping her lips shut, she sat silent, refusing to respond.

Another command in Swahili, and this time Marly saw it coming. She cringed and shifted her head to the side as the big hand with the gnarly knuckles whacked her, this time catching her ear. She teetered in the chair but didn't topple over.

"We could do this all night. Perhaps you need a different kind of incentive." He spoke to the guard by the door, who then turned and left.

"We like to know who is muddying our operations on the continent and who is behind sending covert operatives. Whether you tell us or we find out another way, we will neutralize the problem and continue what we set out to do."

Marly's jaw tightened. "Oh, you mean human trafficking and stealing animals from preserves to sell for profit? You must feel all tough and powerful, preying on those weaker than you."

He chuckled. "It's business. A profitable business."

The man was the lowest of low.

Marly's anger spiked, pushing her to lash out. She lunged forward, tipping the chair enough that she could stand on her feet, albeit at an angle. Then she rushed forward, ramming the desk and hopefully the face of the man responsible for the people and animals trapped in cages.

He scrambled backward, knocking over the chair he'd been sitting on and falling over it to sprawl on the ground.

Marly's momentum carried her onto the table. The legs on one side collapsed and she slid to the ground, landing on her side.

The guard with the killer backhand yanked her up and set her and the chair back where she'd been. He held out his hand to his boss and pulled him to his feet.

Marly's hair hung in her face, obscuring her view of the man in the boonie hat. She wanted to see his face to be able to identify him when she made it back to the authorities. He had to be stopped.

He pulled the hat back in place, shadowing his face again, and set his chair back on its legs but didn't sit. Instead, he walked around the table and stood in front of Marly, wiping blood from his chin. "You will pay for that outburst," he said.

The second guard entered the building, pushing a woman in front of him. She was a beauty, with soulful brown eyes and skin the color of roasted coffee. She'd been crying, the salty traces of tears still evident on her cheeks. She wore a torn business suit incongruous with the rural village.

She spoke in French, appearing to beg the man in charge.

He ignored her pleas and addressed Marly in English. "Ms. Simpson, meet Celeste."

Marly fought to keep from showing any sign of recognition. So this was the woman she'd been talking to on the other side of her cell wall.

"Since you refuse to cooperate with us, Celeste will pay for your obstinacy."

Marly's eyes narrowed. What did he mean?

"Shall we start over?" he asked and continued without waiting for her response. "What are the SEALs doing in Africa?"

"I don't know," Marly said.

Her captor spoke in Swahili.

Celeste's eyes widened and she cried, "No!"

The guard who'd brought her into the building punched her in the gut.

Celeste doubled over and dropped to her knees.

"You dirty bastard!" Marly tried to get up again, but the guard behind her planted his hands on her shoulders and held her down.

"Celeste, darling," the sadistic barbarian

said in a calm and coaxing tone. "Ms. Simpson is the one responsible for your pain. Because she won't answer a few simple questions, you will be punished."

Celeste shook her head, clutching her belly, tears streaming down her cheeks. *"S'il vous plaît. S'il vous plaît."*

Marly's eyes stung. The bile threatened to rise up her throat again. "Don't. She did nothing to deserve this."

"Then tell me what I want to know," the boss said.

Marly swallowed hard. "The SEALs went to Kenya on vacation."

The boss spoke in Swahili. The guard behind Celeste yanked her to her feet and cocked his arm to hit her again.

"No!" Marly yelled. "Don't hit her. Please, don't hurt her. She did nothing. I'm telling the truth. They came for vacation."

"You're lying."

The guard punched Celeste in the belly again. This time, she crumpled and landed on the floor hard, lying as still as death.

Guilt swelled in Marly's chest. "They came for a safari. That's all they came for," she said, tears welling in her eyes.

"Then why did they interfere with my men?" he asked, his voice harsh. "Why were they armed?"

"They didn't come to interfere with your men. But they couldn't stand by and let your men kill the animals and steal their babies. That's just who they are. As far as I know, they're not on a mission. They came to relax." Marly stared at Celeste lying so still on the floor, wondering if the guard had punctured her lung or ruptured her spleen. She prayed the woman was alive.

Even deeper in her heart, she prayed the SEALs would somehow find them and rescue them from this impossible situation.

Chapter Thirteen

Pitbull and his team searched inside and the outer perimeter of the resort compound and past the landing strip. They didn't find any Tangos lying in wait to kill them or take out more guards, but they did find tire tracks in the dust on the far side of the aircraft landing field. They led away and connected to a road leading to and from the resort.

Buck had volunteered to stand guard on the dead men to keep the buzzards from making a meal out of their bodies. Everyone converged on Buck when they'd completed their search.

"Let's go back to the house," Harm said. "Maybe Talia could send the other guard with one of us to the nearest town to ask questions."

Buck nodded toward the house. "Looks like the authorities are finally here." A couple of men in official-looking uniforms strode to-

ward them, followed by four more men carrying two stretchers.

The Kenyan detectives asked questions and
made notes, took pictures and then motioned
for the collection crew to load the bodies onto
the stretchers.

Relieved of their bodyguard duties, the
SEALs returned to the house and the office
where T-Mac was working. The sun was well
on its way toward the horizon, and as far as
Pitbull knew, they still didn't have a clue as
to where Marly and her plane had been taken.

Talia paced the far end of the room, talking
on the satellite phone. When the men entered,
she nodded, acknowledging their presence.
"Look. I need more guards to keep my clients
safe. Do whatever it takes, but have at least
two more out here before midnight."

Pitbull headed straight for T-Mac. "Anything?"

T-Mac held up his hand. "Hang on."

A kernel of hope sat in Pitbull's belly, waiting for whatever T-Mac had to say.

The team's computer guru's fingers flew
across the keyboard as he messaged someone
on the other end of cyberspace.

"Ha!" T-Mac said as he clicked on a link the

other guy provided. A dark screen appeared with numbers, letters and a lot of stuff Pitbull didn't recognize.

"We found the plane," T-Mac said. He pointed to the screen, where sets of numbers and letters flashed. "Our Marly was smart enough to set the transponder code to the hijack frequency 7500."

"How did you know that's the hijack code?" Pitbull asked.

"I told you I had a buddy who knows about airplanes. He helped me download the software that can monitor flights in the area. It took a while, but between the two of us, we found the airplane."

The kernel of hope swelled, filling Pitbull's chest. "Great. Where is she?"

"Looks like she's headed into the Democratic Republic of the Congo."

"Then what are we waiting for?" Pitbull started for the door. "Let's go get her."

T-Mac laughed. "We can't get there on foot. We have to wait for the 160th Night Stalkers to arrive."

As much as Pitbull wanted to be there when they found Marly, he wanted Marly to be safe, first and foremost. "Would it be faster for them to go directly after her?"

"They're in the air now. It might be faster to divert them to her location than to come here first—if we knew where the plane would land."

The blip on the screen blinked, giving Pitbull a little bit of reassurance that the plane was still flying, and Marly could be the pilot, alive and well. Getting to her would be his next hurdle, but as long as she was alive and okay, he could take a moment to be a little relieved.

Except not really. Until she was back with him, safe and sound, he would continue to worry and wish he wasn't so hampered by time and space.

He stared at the monitor, the only lifeline he had between him and Marly.

Suddenly the blip disappeared.

Pitbull's heart leaped into his throat. "What happened?"

"I don't know." T-Mac leaned toward the screen and keyed a message to his friend. Why did it disappear?

The friend instantly sent a message back. Let me check.

T-Mac waited, tapping his fingers on the desktop.

Pitbull paced behind him, his gaze on the monitor, willing the blinking light to reappear.

T-Mac's friend messaged, Either someone turned off the transponder or the engine stopped running.

Pitbull leaned over T-Mac's shoulder, reading the message. "What does he mean, the engine stopped running?"

"They could have landed and shut down the engine." T-Mac glanced up at Pitbull. "The alternative is the plane crashed."

The blood rushed out of Pitbull's head, making him dizzy.

T-Mac touched his arm. "Look, I like Marly as much as you do. Okay, maybe not as much, but I choose to believe they landed."

"Damn—" Pitbull cleared his throat of the knot forming there and started again. "Damn right, they did." He strode toward Talia. "We need to find out where the 160th is and divert them to the plane's last coordinates."

Talia handed him the satellite phone.

"T-Mac, you got those coordinates?" Pitbull demanded.

"Got 'em." T-Mac jotted the numbers on a pad and leaped from the chair.

Pitbull started to place the call to the 160th and stared across the room at Big Jake. "Do it." He handed the phone to his teammate and waited while Big Jake made the call.

A moment later he was in touch with the 160th flight dispatch. "Where did you say they are?" Big Jake held the phone closer, his eyes narrowing. Then his face busted out in a big grin. "Great. Thanks. BJ out." He ended the call and handed the phone to Talia. "Come, on team, we have a flight to catch."

"Where are they?" Pitbull asked.

Big Jake pounded Pitbull on the back. "Landing as we speak."

"Landing where?" Buck asked, yanking the gauze bandage from his head.

"Just outside the compound. Let's go!" Big Jake took off running toward the back of the big house with Pitbull on his heels.

As soon as he exited the building, Pitbull could hear the reassuring thumping of rotor blades beating the air.

They ran through the stand of trees and emerged near the landing strip in a cloud of dust spun up by the two helicopters just touching their skids to the ground.

Pitbull had never been happier to see those helicopters with the gunners hanging out of the side doors, waving for them to climb aboard.

Other members of their team from back at Djibouti were on board, spread out between the two choppers. The men high-fived each other and helped them get settled and strapped in. Once they were all aboard, the helicopters took off.

"They know where we're going?" Pitbull yelled over the roar of the engine and rotor blades.

Big Jake nodded. "They have the coordinates."

As they flew toward Marly, their teammates pulled out weapons and handed them off to Big Jake, Buck and Pitbull. Diesel, Harm and T-Mac would be outfitted similarly on the other chopper. Their unit had been looking out for them. Of course, they'd give them hell about stirring up trouble on their vacation. But that would wait until they got back to Djibouti and they were all sitting around drinking beer.

Pitbull didn't care, as long as they got to Marly in time to save her from the killers who'd taken out two guards to steal her and the plane she flew.

The sun descended to the horizon, slipping lower until it melted into the savanna. Darkness settled in and the stars popped out one by one, filling the sky with a blanket of diamonds.

Marly would have liked watching the sunset from the helicopter, and then she would have told him how much she liked viewing the sky without all the light pollution of the big cities. If he got her back…

Pitbull shook his head. No. *When* he got her back, he'd still have to let her go. She'd want to stay in Africa, and he had a job based out of Virginia. Hell, that bridge he needed to cross was coming far too fast. First things first, though. He had to get Marly back.

He wished he could fly in the cockpit as he had with Marly. At least then he could see where they were going and get a feeling for how much farther they had left to travel. Marly's plane had flown for a few hours. To catch up to them, they'd have to fly for as long, maybe longer. He wasn't sure how fast

Marly's plane flew, but it had to be faster than the Black Hawk helicopters.

Pitbull stared hard at the front of the aircraft, willing it to fly faster than it had ever flown before. The sooner they got to Marly, the better.

BECAUSE CELESTE HAD passed out, the boss decided to slap Marly around some more until she couldn't see straight and barely hung on to consciousness. Finally, she let her head droop and half feigned unconsciousness. One more hit and she'd be out, but really, she could care less if they hit her as long as they took her back to the holding cell she'd left. At least there she had a chance of escaping. And she'd get Celeste out, even if she had to carry her out herself.

When the boss got bored with slapping her around, he waved to the guards, spoke in their language and then got up to leave.

The guards tossed the women over their shoulders like sacks of potatoes and carried them back to their respective cells.

Thankfully, Marly ended up in the one she'd worked on so hard. She was glad she'd done the work before they'd beaten her. After the way they'd treated her, she wasn't sure she would have had the strength to dig all those holes in the wall. She wasn't even sure she'd be able to climb up the wall and push her way through the thatch with her vision blurring and pain shooting through her head.

Once the guards dropped her on the ground, she lay there for a few minutes, listening to the sound of their boots as they walked away. When she was sure they were gone, she dragged herself to her feet and leaned her head against the wall. "Celeste."

No response.

"Celeste, please wake up."

A moan sounded through the wall.

"That's it. Wake up. I'm going to try to get out of here. Be ready for when I come to get you."

"Non," she said softly in her lovely French accent. *"Je ne peux pas.* I cannot."

"Yes, you can. If I can get out, you can come with me. You have to help me get the others out. I can't do it alone."

Silence stretched for a few moments. Marly thought Celeste had slipped into unconsciousness again.

Then Celeste spoke. "I will be ready."

Strengthened by the knowledge Celeste wasn't dead or still out cold, Marly stood, fought back dizziness and climbed to the top of the wall. The underwire from her bra still hung in the thatch. She used it again to hack away at the thatch bindings, putting everything she had into the effort, finally breaking through.

Parting the thick grasses used to make the thatch proved to be harder. Dirt, dust and mildew had fused the strands together. She cut through it with the wire and despaired of ever seeing the stars again.

Suddenly the thatch parted and she could see clear sky with a plethora of twinkling diamonds shining down at her. A rush of tears stung her eyes. She blinked them back and continued widening the hole until she could fit her shoulders into it. Then she pulled her torso through, braced her feet on the wall below and pushed the rest of her body out. With her calves and ankles still trapped, she swayed, drinking in fresh air and freedom.

Footsteps crunching on gravel made her hunker close to the roofline. Below, a guard walked by, carrying a semiautomatic rifle slung over his shoulder, the barrel pointed at the ground. He appeared bored, his feet shuffling pebbles as he moved past.

Marly waited until he was out of sight around the corner of another structure before she pulled her feet out of the thatch. No sooner had she gotten them out than she fell backward, landing on the slick grass and sliding toward the edge of the roof.

She twisted, rolling onto her stomach and reaching out to grab hold of something, anything. The blades of grass used to make the thatch slipped through her fingers. She couldn't find purchase and plummeted to the ground.

Her feet hit first, her knees buckled and she fell back on her buttocks with a hard thump. The jolt didn't feel good on her backside, but nothing was broken and she was still conscious. She'd consider that a success.

Resting on her laurels wasn't a luxury she could afford. The guard could come back through at any moment, and she still had to get Celeste and any other women who might be held captive out of their cells.

Marly jumped to her feet and ran around the hut to the other side. The building stretched fifty feet to her left. She'd been in the outer cell with Celeste next to her. The doors were made of rough planks with rudimentary boards dropped into place, effectively locking the door without a lock.

Marly nearly cried out with excitement. Her luck was just beginning to change. Quickly she shoved the board up on Celeste's cell and swung the door open.

Celeste fell through and hugged her hard. *"Merci beaucoup,"* she whispered, hugging her again.

Marly closed Celeste's door and shifted the board back into the locked position. The guards wouldn't think they'd escaped if the doors were still closed and locked. She turned to the other woman. "There are more?"

Celeste nodded and pointed to the other doors. "They were in there."

Each taking a different door, they worked their way along the front of the building. After they'd freed two others, Marly positioned Celeste at the corner of the building to watch for the return of the guard. Marly and the freed women continued to empty the cells. Once they had all the women out, they huddled in the shadows between the long building that had been their prison and another whose roof had caved in and appeared to be abandoned. Counting Marly, there were ten women.

"Do you know if there is an aircraft landing strip near here?" Marly asked Celeste.

Celeste shook her head. "I do not know. I woke up here." She turned to some of the others and spoke in Swahili.

One woman nodded and pointed.

"She says they brought her in tonight on a road in that direction. She saw an airplane out there."

Marly's heart skipped a few beats, excitement building. They might have a chance to escape yet.

The scuffle of footsteps on the gravel had all ten women freezing in place. Marly pressed a finger to her lips. Hiding one person wasn't as big a deal as hiding a gaggle of females.

The bored guard walked past the gap between buildings where the women hid. Marly's eyes narrowed. She recognized him as the one to punch Celeste in the belly so many times.

One of the younger women gasped.

Marly froze in a crouched position. If she had to, she'd attack. She prayed it didn't come to that.

The guard paused halfway past the gap. As if in slow motion, he turned toward the women.

He didn't have time to raise his weapon before Marly sprang forward and hit him in the gut like a linebacker going after the quarterback. The man fell to the ground, the air knocked from his lungs.

Marly straddled him, pinning his arms to the ground, his weapon trapped between them.

Celeste slapped her hand over his mouth and said something in Swahili. One of the women grabbed a knife from a scabbard on the man's belt and slammed it into the man's chest.

It all happened so fast, Marly didn't have time to process what had just occurred. They'd killed a guard.

Holy hell. When the boss found out, he'd kill all of them.

Marly decided then and there that the boss couldn't find out. Not until they were long gone from there and on their way to freedom.

"Grab an arm," she said to Celeste. Together, they dragged the man into the abandoned building and left him in the deepest shadows. He wouldn't be found until the next day, if that soon. He might rot before they discovered him from the smell. As far as Marly was concerned, he deserved to rot in hell. He'd nearly killed Celeste. The only man worse than him was the one who'd ordered him to hit defenseless Celeste.

Once the guard was stashed in the dark, Marly grabbed his rifle and peered out of the abandoned building, watching for any other movement. At the far end of the camp, close to the building she'd been interrogated in, lights came on and an engine fired up. It sounded like the diesel engine of a big truck. Men carried cages and crates to the trucks, loading them one at a time.

Nobody came in their direction. They appeared to be concentrating on loading the truck. Marly guessed they were loading the animals, ready to ship them off for sale. She wished she could help them, but first she had to get the women to safety. Then she'd come back with Pitbull and his team and kill every one of the murdering, stealing, human-trafficking bastards.

Now would be the time if they were going to make a run for it. The truck's engine noise would mask the sound of the airplane engine starting up, buying them time to get away.

Marly motioned for the women to stay put. She ran to the corner of the next building, keeping to the shadows. With the lights shining at the other end of camp, hopefully the men would be night-blind and miss the movements of ten women escaping.

Marly shot a glance left and right. So far, the area was free of guards. She waved for the women to follow. When they were on their way toward her, she ran to the corner of the next building and the next until she stood at the edge of the village near the road the truck would have to travel to get out.

Two hundred yards away, gleaming silvery blue in the moonlight, stood Marly's plane. Parked close beside it were two tanker trucks, presumably containing gasoline or diesel for the trucks. What were the chances they were filled with aviation fuel? Slim to none. She prayed there was enough fuel left to get the plane and ten women off the ground and to the nearest airport with available fuel.

She was about to make a run across the wide-open expanse when a four-wheel-drive vehicle pulled out of the village and parked near her plane.

"No, no, no," she whispered.

"What?" Celeste moved up beside her.

"Please don't take the plane," she whispered.

Celeste's breath caught on a gasp. "That is him." She pointed toward the man getting out of the vehicle.

The boonie hat gave him away.

Marly's blood boiled and she nearly shouted out to the man who'd orchestrated what was happening to them. He walked toward the plane and pulled the steps down.

"He can't get away," Marly said through gritted teeth. "Not in my plane. Not in anything."

"He cannot be allowed to continue," Celeste said.

Marly lifted the rifle to her shoulder. "I won't let this happen." She'd fired rifles before, but never something like the one she'd pilfered from the dead guard. At two hundred yards, she doubted she'd hit the man. But he couldn't be allowed to get away. Lives were at risk. The futures of other women were hanging in the balance.

Knowing she'd never hit such a small target as a man at two hundred yards' distance, she did the only other thing she could, fully understanding the ramifications if she succeeded.

Chapter Fourteen

The 160th Night Stalkers set down the helicopters on the other side of a hill, a couple miles from the exact coordinates they'd been given of the last known location of Marly's plane. Two miles was a lot of ground to cover, but they couldn't risk giving Marly's captors a heads-up that they were on their way in.

With communications headsets on and M4A1 rifles locked and loaded, they scrambled out of the aircraft and hurried toward their destination.

Pitbull led the way, holding the GPS device with the coordinates keyed in. He didn't slow for a moment, pushing harder and faster than he'd ever pushed in his life. Lights ahead made him slow to a stop.

"Harm, cover me should anyone enter from outside this point," he ordered.

Harm was the second-best shot on the team next to Pitbull. In reality, Pitbull should be covering for the rest of the team, but he had to go in and find Marly. He would be less than useless providing cover when his heart and soul were trapped somewhere inside the village in front of him.

Harm got in position and raised his rifle to his shoulder. "Got your six," he said in Pitbull's headset.

Pitbull waved to Buck and Big Jake. "Follow me."

Big Jake motioned to the others. "Everyone else spread out on the perimeter and take out guards and sentries."

The men fanned out, circling the compound while Pitbull headed in, Big Jake and Buck close behind. Once Pitbull reached the first building, he pushed open the door and entered, shining his penlight around an empty room. He exited and waved for Big Jake and Buck to make their move while Pitbull provided cover.

Big Jake and Buck hugged the shadows and moved to the next building, securing it before they gave Pitbull the thumbs-up.

Bright lights lit up the night outside a larger

building ahead. A truck was positioned outside the structure, and men were hurriedly loaded boxes and crates into the back. The sounds of animals screaming and screeching added to a sense of chaos and desperation.

Big Jake squatted in the shadows, raised his rifle to his shoulder and waited.

Buck and Pitbull bounded forward, pushed past Big Jake's position and moved on to the next building, a long mud-and-stick building with a thatched roof and doors lining the front. One by one, Pitbull and Buck checked inside each door. Pitbull almost missed it when he glanced in the last one on the end, but something caught his eye as he flashed his penlight around the room. Hanging from the corner ceiling was a bra. A pretty pink one, exactly like the one Marly had been wearing beneath her flight suit the day she'd pulled out her handgun.

"Buck," Pitbull whispered into his headset. "Come see this."

Buck entered the room behind him and shone his light at the pink bra stuck in the ceiling.

"See that hole in the thatch?" Pitbull chuckled and pointed his light at the corner where grooves had been scraped into the wall. He climbed halfway up the wall, snagged the bra and stuffed it into the cargo pocket in his pants. "She escaped."

"That's our Marly." Buck backed out of the building. "But where to?"

"Knowing her, she's going for her airplane. Anyone see a plane yet?"

"T-Mac here. We haven't made it completely around the west perimeter yet. No sign of an airplane on my side."

One of the other men reported in, "I'm only halfway around the east side. No sign of a plane yet."

"We came in from the south," Big Jake said. "Maybe it's on the north."

"Right," Pitbull said. "We're working our way around the interior." He exited the hut and provided cover while Big Jake and Buck advanced this time. They were getting closer to the men loading crates and cages onto the trucks.

"We found the stolen animals," Buck said. "They're all babies and they're loading them into the trucks."

"Any sign of Marly?" Pitbull asked.

"No," Big Jake said. "Covering."

Pitbull hurried forward, hiding in the shadows a little ahead of where Big Jake and Buck were positioned. He was worried about Marly. If she'd escaped and been recaptured, they might have been harder on her. Maybe they put her in one of the cages being loaded onto the truck. Until they checked all the outer buildings, he couldn't go there.

Though it frustrated him to no end, Pitbull continued the search. They cleared all the buildings except those nearest the trucks and the hive of activity. A smaller vehicle pulled away, heading to the north, away from the light and the truck.

By that time, they'd made a complete circle inside the village and were on the southeastern side, close to the trucks.

"Found your plane," T-Mac said in Pitbull's ear.

Pitbull was so elated, he nearly stepped out of the shadows. "Where?" he said past the knot in his chest.

"North end, a couple hundred yards from the village. There's a road out here. That's probably what they landed on."

"How close are you?"

"Three hundred yards. It's sitting out in the open."

"Any lights on the inside? Anyone moving around it?"

"No lights, no movement. Wait. A vehicle just came out of the village. It's stopping in front of the plane."

Pitbull was already moving north.

"Pitbull, maintain situational awareness," Big Jake warned him.

Pitbull slowed, realizing he was out in the open. Any person who was a decent shot could take him out with one bullet. Then they'd know they'd been infiltrated. His team would be at risk.

Pitbull pulled himself together and ducked back into the shadows, raised his weapon and waited for Big Jake and Buck to move.

Buck let Big Jake go ahead. "You all right?" Buck asked.

Pitbull gave Buck a thumbs-up. "Ready?"

Big Jake dropped to one knee and waited for Buck and Pitbull to bound ahead.

Just when he stepped out of the shadows, Pitbull heard a burst of gunfire. A moment later, an explosion ripped through the air.

"What the hell?" Pitbull stared to the north

where a fireball rose into the sky, lighting the ground below.

With huts between him and the edge of the village, he couldn't see where the fire was coming from.

"Damn," a voice came across the mic. "We better hope Marly wasn't headed for her plane."

"Why?" Pitbull ditched protocol and started running toward the fireball. "Why, damn it?"

"The fireball?" T-Mac paused. "Was her plane."

As if a giant fist slugged him in the gut, Pitbull stumbled and fell to his knees.

Buck raced up behind him and helped him to his feet. "She wasn't in it."

"How do you know?" Pitbull looked up at his friend. "She would have gone to her plane."

"Maybe she was caught. Maybe she's waiting for us to rescue her." Buck dragged Pitbull toward the side of a building. "You can't give up hope now."

"That was her plane." Pitbull shook his head. "She loved that plane."

"Yeah, well, we have different problems

now." Buck jerked his head in the direction from which they'd come.

Pitbull glanced toward the lights and the trucks. The people who'd been loading the crates and cages were running in their direction.

"Look out, gang. All hell's about to break loose," Pitbull said into the mic.

"Hunker down and hold your fire. No one shoots until the first shot is fired," Big Jake said.

The men running toward them were armed with rifles and machine guns.

Someone fired shots, and like a chain reaction, bullets flew.

Pitbull waited as long as he could, but when the men came within two yards of him, he opened fire. One of the advancing men fired at Pitbull, hitting the wall of the building behind him, barely missing his head.

Big Jake took the enemy out with one shot to the forehead.

When they saw their buddies dropping, the men in the rear turned around and ran in the other direction, climbing into whatever smaller, faster vehicle they could find. Moments later, the night grew silent but for the sound of engines fading into the distance.

"Perimeter check," Big Jake said.

"All clear."

"Bring it in. Go door to door," Pitbull said, his voice dull, his heart no longer into the mission. He stared at the flames leaping into the sky.

"Is that a fuel truck next to the plane?" Buck pointed at a vehicle as the tires caught fire.

"Holy crap!" Pitbull exclaimed.

At that moment, the tanker truck exploded, knocking Pitbull back on his heels. His head reverberated from the concussion, and he couldn't hear past the ringing in his ears.

"No sign of Marly in the big truck or any of the crates or cages on board," T-Mac reported in.

Pitbull could barely hear through the roar in his head.

"Buildings are empty. Everyone left. No sign of Marly," Diesel reported minutes later.

Pitbull pushed to his feet and stared at the wreckage. "Marly, baby. I'm sorry. I should have been there for you."

Buck came up behind him and laid a hand

on his shoulder. He spoke slowly and clearly. "She wasn't in the plane."

"But she was here." He pulled the pink bra from his back pocket. "She was here."

"But she's not here now." Buck nodded toward the plane. "And she wasn't in the plane. You have to believe that."

"I never should have let her go back for her logbook. It could have waited." Pitbull shook his head. "I'm so sorry, Marly. I wish I had never let you out of my sight."

MARLY HAD PULLED the trigger, determined to keep the boss from getting away with all the atrocities he'd committed. She had no idea how long his operation had been in business, or how many women he'd sold into slavery. All she knew was he couldn't be allowed to continue.

She aimed the rifle at the man and shifted to the fuel truck closest to the plane.

"Tell the women to duck and hold their ears," she warned Celeste.

Celeste translated and lay down with her face to the ground, her hands over her ears. The other ladies followed suit.

"Sorry, baby," Marly said to her plane and

pulled the trigger, holding it long enough to release a burst of bullets. Seconds later, the world rocked with the explosion. She was knocked backward, where she hit her head on a tree and passed out.

How long she lay in the dark, she didn't know. When she came to, she sat up. Her ears rang and her head hurt. A ball of fire rose from what was left of her plane and the fuel truck. Her heart hurt, but she couldn't regret her decision.

Men's voices sounded nearby and they were speaking English, but she couldn't make out the words. Her ears rang too loud, and she didn't have a whole lot of control of her motor movements.

When she finally pushed to her feet, another explosion ripped through the air, again knocking her to the ground. She lay still. The stars she could see through the trees blurred and faded to black.

When she surfaced again, she blinked up at tree branches and more stars. Her ears were still ringing, but her vision was beginning to clear. She moved her fingers and toes, then her legs and arms. Nothing hurt, other than the bruises she'd received from her captors.

Then she remembered the nine other women she'd been trying to get to safety.

Marly sat up too fast. Her head spun, but she pushed past the dizziness, refusing to pass out again.

The women lay on the ground around her. Some sobbed quietly, while others lay with their hands over their ears as if waiting for the next explosion.

Celeste pushed to a sitting position beside her and blinked.

"Are you all right?" Marly asked.

Celeste nodded and winced. "My ears hurt and I can't hear well."

"That would be a concussion from the explosion. Hopefully, it will go away soon."

She stared out at the plane and fuel trucks. "Did you get him?"

Marly nodded. "Nobody could have lived through that explosion. You felt it from here and we're over two hundred yards away."

Celeste nodded. "Still, I want to see the body. Proof."

Marly understood. She, too, wanted proof the man died in the explosion, never to torture, sell or trade in humans and animals ever again.

Now that they were free of him, would they be able to get away from the others? She'd destroyed their means of transportation, and going back to where the others had been loading trucks would be a very bad idea.

Marly glanced at the road leading away from the village. They might have to walk. "Let's ask the others if they can walk."

Celeste and Marly went around to each of the women to make sure they were okay. Some were so distraught, they couldn't stop crying. Others sat in shock, almost catatonic. All of them seemed physically well enough to walk, though.

Marly glanced back at the village. A light still burned near the other end where the trucks had been and the animals had been loaded. The engine noise had ceased, and she couldn't make out any shouts. Then she remembered hearing voices before the last explosion. Voices speaking English. American English.

Her pulse sped up, and she pushed to her feet. "Keep them here. I want to check on something."

Celeste grabbed her wrist. "It is too dangerous."

"I'll be careful. If don't come back in five

minutes, take the women and start walking. Follow the road, but don't walk on it. Stay in the shadows and move at night. Understand?"

Celeste nodded. "Please don't go."

Marly squeezed her hand. "I have to." Deep in her heart, she knew she'd heard something. Had it been a dream? Had she had a flashback to her time spent at the All Things Wild Resort? Or were there really men here who spoke American English? And if there were, who were they and what were they doing here?

Marly stood and walked toward the village, moving from tree to tree, still a little wobbly on her legs. Her hearing was coming back slowly. She could swear she heard the murmur of voices. She worked her way toward them and came to a stop when she heard one very familiar tone.

"I'm so sorry, Marly." The voice came from the shadows beneath a tree. "I wish I had never let you out of my sight."

Her heart skipped several beats and then raced, pounding so hard against her eardrums, she was afraid she would lose her hearing altogether.

"Pitbull?" she whispered. Then she was running, crashing through the trees. "Pitbull?"

"Marly?" A man materialized out of the shadows, caught her in his arms and crushed her to his chest. "Oh, Marly, I thought you were gone. I thought I'd lost you in that explosion."

"You found me," Marly said. "I can't believe you found me."

"I'd have searched to the ends of the earth. I never should have let you go back to your plane alone."

She cupped his cheek and leaned up on her toes to lightly kiss his lips, her heart so full she thought her chest might explode. "You found me."

Pitbull held her close, his lips crashing down on hers.

Marly winced and jerked back.

"Did I hurt you?" Pitbull held her at arm's length.

She touched her hand to her mouth. "I have a split lip. But I don't care. Kiss me again." She pressed her mouth to his, but he refused to kiss her.

Instead, he raised a penlight and scanned her face and body. "Sweet Jesus, Marly, what did they do to you? Are you bleeding?" He shone his light over the blood stains on her flight suit. "Buck! We need a medic! Stat!"

She touched his cheek again and shook her head. "I'm okay but for a few bumps and bruises. This blood isn't mine."

"Not yours?" He let go of a long, heavy sigh.

"No, it was the guard who gave me these." She pointed to her bruised cheekbone and jaw.

"Dead, I hope?"

She nodded. "Very."

By the fierce look on Pitbull's face, the dead man was lucky the SEAL hadn't gotten to him first. He'd have made him suffer for hurting Marly.

Pitbull didn't belabor the discussion of the man's death, which suited Marly fine. She still wasn't sure how she felt about killing. Though she hadn't killed the man who'd hit her, she had been responsible for the death of his sadistic boss.

She shook off the thought and hugged Pitbull again. "How did you find me?"

Buck appeared behind Pitbull. "Actually, T-Mac found you and we all came to rescue you. Poor Pitbull was so distraught, we were surprised he didn't catch your plane with his bare hands before it left the ground. If he could have run eighty miles per hour, he might have done it."

"I saw you," she said. "And I couldn't do anything about it. They threatened to kill all of you with a grenade. I had to fly." She pressed her cheek to his. "And then the bastards pulled me out of the pilot's seat and knocked me out."

Pitbull's arms tightened around her waist. "I'm sorry you had to go through that. I'd kill them all over again if I could."

"All over again?" Marly glanced around. That's when she saw the bodies lying on the ground. "Are these the men who were working this operation?"

Pitbull nodded.

Her gaze shifted to Pitbull's. "They were trading in baby animals and human trafficking."

"Human trafficking?" Big Jake shook his head. "Death was too good for them."

She nodded in the direction of the women hiding in the woods. "Celeste, you can come out now. It's safe."

Moments later, the nine women walked out of the woods, following the sound of Marly's voice.

They held back when they saw Pitbull, Big Jake and Buck's big, burly bodies surrounding Marly.

"Don't worry, they're here to rescue us." Marly hurried over to Celeste, took her arm and walked her over to the men. "This is Celeste. She helped me get all the women out."

Celeste nodded. "Thank you for coming to help us."

Big Jake chuckled. "It appears you didn't need us, after all."

Marly raised her eyebrows and stared around at the men littering the ground. "We would be dead if you hadn't come. These men would have killed us after I took out their boss."

Pitbull frowned. "You took out their boss?"

She tipped her head toward the smoldering fire. "I sacrificed my plane rather than let him get away in it."

"You were responsible for the explosion?" Buck asked.

Marly nodded. "I couldn't let the man behind this operation get away. He would have gone on to kill more animals and kidnap more women, only to sell them to the highest bidders. I couldn't let him do that." She shook her head, staring at the smoldering heap. "I'd do it all over again."

T-Mac, Harm and Diesel joined them, each giving Marly a huge hug.

"We weren't sure we'd find you," Harm said.

T-Mac backhanded Harm in the gut. "What are you talking about? It was only a matter of time before I located her. I had no doubt in my mind we'd find our Marly." He frowned at the fire. "I'm sorry about your plane."

She shrugged and slipped her arm around Pitbull's waist. "I'm just glad you guys are okay." Marly frowned. "By the way, how'd you get here?"

Pitbull grinned. "Our unit sent helicopters."

"Oh, dear Lord. You flew in one of those death traps?" She winked. "Well, I'm glad you didn't crash."

"I'm sure the 160th will appreciate the sentiment," Big Jake said. "Speaking of which, I put in a call for extraction. They should be here in just a minute."

Pitbull pulled her close and held her tight.

Marly turned in Pitbull's arms. "But we can't leave."

"What do you mean? We're in the Democratic Republic of the Congo without permission. As far as you and anyone else are concerned, we aren't here," Pitbull said.

"But the crates." Marly grabbed Pitbull's hand and dragged him toward the light in the center of the village.

"Where are we going?" he asked.

"We have to take care of the animals."

"We can't airlift them out of the Congo," Pitbull said.

"No, but we can drive them out," Marly said. "The men loaded them into the trucks. All we have to do is drive them east back into Kenya and take them to a sanctuary where someone can care for the babies until they're old enough to be on their own."

Pitbull chuckled. "You make it sound so easy."

"What's hard about it?" Marly stared around at the men in the night, their eyes shining by the light of the moon. "They got them here by truck. We should be able to get them out the same way."

Pitbull looked over her head at Big Jake. "What do you say? Want to pull an all-nighter and get the kids to a safe place?"

"I'm game," Buck said.

Big Jake drew in a deep breath and let it out. "We're already in hot water for being in the DRC when we're supposed to be in Kenya. We should let the crew get the women home, and those of us on *vacation* can get the trucks loaded with animals and headed somewhere safe, where they won't die or be sold."

The helicopters flew in just then, landing on the road a couple hundred yards away from the dying fire. The SEAL team, minus the six who'd chosen a relaxing vacation in Kenya, escorted the women to the helicopters.

Pitbull bent to kiss Marly's lips. "You need to go with the women."

Marly shook her head. "I'm going with you."

"As much as I'd love to have you with me, I know those women need a strong lady like you to make them feel more comfortable flying off with a bunch of men. Especially after what they've been through."

Marly frowned. He was right. She hadn't gotten them this far just to abandon them. "Promise me you'll be okay if I don't go with you."

He held up a hand. "I promise." Pitbull pressed his lips to the top of her head. "You know I'd have given anything to see you go all commando and blow up your plane."

She smiled. "You have no idea how hard it was to pull that trigger."

"Oh, baby, I do. I know how much you loved that plane." He hugged her one last time and then escorted her to the waiting helicopters. "Now, don't jinx the pilot. This helicopter is perfectly safe and won't drop out of the sky. I'll see you soon."

"You bet." She climbed aboard, turned and threw him a kiss. Then she was being hustled into a harness, and the helicopter lifted off the ground.

As the chopper rose into the air, Marly focused on the man who'd changed her life and made her feel like a woman, not just a grease-jockey pilot.

Soon he became a speck and all she could see was the plume of smoke that had once been her plane.

Her heart hurt. Her plane had been like a friend. The decision to destroy it hadn't been easy. But now that it was done, what could she do with her life? The possibilities were dauntingly endless.

First, she had to get these women to safety.

Sure, the SEALs could have done it without her, but the ladies had been through so much at the hands of ruthless men. Having another female around would help calm their fears in the transition.

Marly smiled. Most of them had never flown in a helicopter. In the limited light from the helicopter control panel and from the starlight, she could see the terror in their faces. As much as she wanted to be with Pitbull at that moment, she'd made the right decision to fly with the freed captives.

The big question in her mind was what would happen next between her and Pitbull?

Chapter Fifteen

Once Marly's helicopter disappeared into the night sky, Pitbull hurried to the trucks the men had been loading. The animals in the cages and crates were showing signs of extreme stress. Many of the babies had probably gone without nourishment for far too long. The best they could do for them was to get them to a rehabilitation sanctuary as soon as possible.

The men finished loading the last few crates and cages. After a final check around the village for any remaining animals or people, the men piled into the trucks and headed out, wanting to make good use of darkness to get out of the DRC and back into Kenya.

The roads were rough. Pitbull worried about the animals in the back. The men didn't have the supplies or the knowledge of each creature to stop and feed them, or he would have.

Still, they were better off than being abandoned in the village to die of starvation and dehydration.

The SEALs pushed on, finally crossing into Kenya as the sun popped up from the eastern horizon.

Big Jake had contacted Talia via the satellite phone the team had brought for them. She had arranged for the delivery of the animals to a refuge fifty miles into Kenya. They were greeted by an army of volunteers who helped unload the animals, sort them and place them into better environments.

Pitbull and his teammates stayed to help care for the baby animals until all had been fed and housed. Every one of the creatures survived the trip, some in better shape than others.

By the time they left the sanctuary, the men had been awake for over forty-eight hours. They were exhausted, hungry and in need of a full day's sleep. Still, they pushed on, driving the trucks they'd taken from the illegal compound, finally reaching the All Things Wild Resort as the sun rose on a fresh day.

Talia greeted them in front the big house in her khaki uniform, her hair perfectly combed, a frown pulling her eyebrows together. "Tell me you got some sleep along the way."

Big Jake rubbed a hand across his three-day-old beard. "No, ma'am. And I'm sure we smell like the animals we rescued."

"Go get yourselves cleaned up. I'll have food on the table in ten minutes." She paused. "Unless you'd prefer to sleep first."

As one, the men said, "Food."

She smiled. "Then food it is." Talia turned toward the house.

Before she disappeared through the door, Pitbull called out, "Any word from Marly?"

Talia shook her head. "Sorry. I've heard nothing."

Big Jake laid a hand on Pitbull's shoulder. "The 160th wasn't supposed to be in the DRC or in Kenya. I'm sure they had to fly low on the radar, literally and figuratively. Marly will contact us as soon as she is able."

"It's been more than twenty-four hours." Pitbull scrubbed a hand over his tired face. "Talia, I won't be at the breakfast table. I'd rather get sleep."

"I can have someone deliver a tray to your bungalow, if you don't feel like coming to the big house," she offered.

"No, thank you." He walked away, heading for his assigned cabin. Once inside, he closed the door and leaned his forehead against the wood paneling. As tired as he was, he couldn't stop thinking about Marly. He had to tell himself she was in good hands, free of the man who'd dared to deal in humans and animals.

She must be hurting, possibly scared. Without her plane, what did her future hold for her?

Pitbull wished he could scoop her into his arms and tell her everything would be all right.

As he walked to the bathroom, he stripped out of his dirty clothing, letting the items fall to the floor along the way. He switched on the shower and stood in the spray for almost half an hour, his body and mind so drained he could barely remember to work up a lather and scrub the dirt out of his hair and skin.

When he finished, he dried himself, wrapped the towel around his waist and walked into the bedroom.

A tray piled high with breakfast foods sat in the middle of the bed.

His stomach rumbled loudly.

"How long has it been since you've eaten?"

a familiar voice asked from the adjoining sitting room.

Pitbull spun toward the sound, his heart banging hard against his ribs. "Marly."

She stood framed in the doorway, wearing a long, colorful caftan cinched at the waist, her sandy-blond hair hanging long and loose down her back.

"Miss me much?" she asked, not making a move toward him.

"You have no clue," he whispered.

She chuckled, the sound warming the air between them. "Then give me one."

He opened his arms and she walked into them. "I haven't stopped thinking about you since we left Djibouti on our way to a little vacation safari in Kenya."

She rested her cheek against his chest. "Your heart is beating so fast."

He cupped the back of her head and pressed a kiss to her forehead. "I missed you, Marly Simpson. When I thought I'd lost you, I realized just how much you've become a part of my life."

"In a very short amount of time," she added, tipping her head up to stare into his eyes. "Do you believe in love at first sight?" she asked.

He shook his head. "No. But I believe in love at last." He framed her face in his palms and bent to brush his mouth lightly over her lips. "I don't want to hurt you."

"I trust that you won't," she said.

He knew she was talking about more than the cut on her lip or the bruises on her jaw and cheeks. "Where are you going from here, Marly? Will you get another plane and continue your flying service?"

She tilted her head to the side. "I don't think so."

"No?" His pulse beat a little faster, hope taking root in his heart.

"I haven't been back to where I was born in a very long time. Do you think they have need of pilots in my home state of Virginia?" She smiled up at him. "Not that I'm asking for strings attached or commitment, but it would be nice to try my hand at dating again. I feel as if I haven't given it enough of a chance."

He laughed and kissed the spot on her face that had the least amount of deep purple bruising. "I think you'll love it, as long as you're dating the right man."

"It all depends on whether he bucks up enough courage to ask me."

"Oh, I can guarantee he'll ask you. But in the meantime, we have a few more days of vacation left here at All Things Wild. Anything special you want to do before we leave?"

She walked her fingers up his chest and pressed one to his lips. "I can think of a few things I'd like to accomplish."

"Accomplish? That sounds like work."

"Seriously, I'd like to find out who else was involved in the human trafficking and the animal sales. The man in charge of that little operation was American. He could have had a partner stateside, facilitating the sales to the US or on to other countries."

Pitbull tucked a strand of Marly's hair back behind her ear. "I agree. We need to find out who else was involved in the trafficking ring." He circled his hands around her waist and then slid them lower to cup her bottom. "Can you think of anything else you'd like to accomplish before we leave?"

She ran her tongue across her lips and smiled. "I'd like to get better at the art of seduction." She stared up at him. "Do you know anyone willing to teach me? I'd really like to become an accomplished flirt."

"I might know a guy." He brushed his

thumb over her swollen lip. Pitbull moved closer, reached down and released the towel around his waist. "Anything else you'd like to do before we leave?"

"Oh, yeah. There is something you should know." She leaned up on her toes and whispered in his ear. "I'm going commando. There's absolutely nothing but me underneath this dress."

Pitbull's hands tightened around her waist. "Marly, you're an amazing woman. You don't need lessons in flirting. You already know exactly what to say and do to capture my interest." He gathered the fabric of her dress and pulled it up and over her head, then tossed it to a chair in the corner.

"Don't you want to eat breakfast?" she asked as she slid into his arms, pressing her naked flesh to his.

"Later, babe. I have you in my arms. I don't want to waste a second."

"Oh, good. But we can eat later, can't we? I think we'll be starved by then."

"You've got it, but first, I want to hold you like there will be no tomorrow. To feel your body next to mine and to make love to you all day and all night long."

"I've never heard of anything sweeter. Maybe I'm getting the hang of this seduction thing. It seems to be working on you."

He touched a finger to the tip of her nose. "Hold that thought and don't move." Then he stepped away from her, gathered the tray of food, set it on the table in the sitting room and returned.

Marly hadn't moved. She stood as naked as he'd left her, wearing nothing but a smile.

She was long, lean and perfect in every way. He couldn't imagine any other woman he'd rather be with or have in his life.

"Are you going to stand there staring at me all night long, or make love to me?"

Pitbull laughed, swept her up into his arms and carried her to the king-size bed, where he laid her down gently.

He lay on the bed beside her and gathered her in his arms. "I don't know what will happen when we leave here or how our relationship will progress, but I know one thing."

"What's that?" Marly asked, leaning over to press her lips to his.

"I want you in my life with all the strings attached and a heaping helping of commitment. You're an amazing woman, strong, selfless and independent—everything I never knew I wanted in the woman I can see myself spending the rest of my life with."

"Wow," Marly said. "Just days ago, you were dead set against relationships. As a SEAL, you would never be around. Relationships never work, you said." She tipped her head to the side. "What made you change your mind?"

"You, baby. The person you are. The unassuming way you go about your life. Your fierce independence. If anyone can put up with the life of a SEAL, baby, it's you. You gave me hope for a future I never thought I'd have."

Marly frowned. "I don't know. I'm not anything special."

"You're wrong. You're the best thing to ever happen to me. I don't need a year of dating to come to that conclusion. I know now, you're the one for me. But if you want to date and take your time to come to the same conclusion, I'll do whatever it takes. As long as you end up in my arms, in my life and in my heart."

Marly moved closer, pressing the length of her body against the length of his. "I don't need a year to know what's already in my heart. It's you. Are we clear now? We care about each other and don't want it to end after we leave here."

He chuckled and kissed the tip of her nose. "We're clear."

"Good, because I'd like to stop talking and start loving."

"Bossy much?" he said, pulling her closer. He bent to kiss her lips, ever so softly. "Who knew a vacation could end up being a new beginning?"

"I like to think I keep an open mind. Now, shut up and make love to me."

* * * * *

Get 4 FREE REWARDS!

We'll send you 2 FREE Books plus 2 FREE Mystery Gifts.

Harlequin Presents® books feature a sensational and sophisticated world of international romance where sinfully tempting heroes ignite passion.

FREE
Value Over
$20

Get 4 FREE REWARDS!

We'll send you 2 FREE Books plus 2 FREE Mystery Gifts.

FREE Value Over **$20**

Both the **Romance** and **Suspense** collections feature compelling novels written by many of today's best-selling authors.